THE ASSASSIN OF THE STORM

Book 1 of Shattering Skies

JAMES SABBINI

CHAPTER 1

Zephyros stood at the cliff's edge, his heart heavy with unease as he peered into the chasm below. The wind, cold and relentless, whipped his long silver hair across his face, a reminder of the storm brewing both within him and beyond.

Below him, the Valley of Aetheros stretched out like a sea of green, stippled with the bright gold lights of his village that nestled among the hills. The sun was setting, casting an amber glow over the land he had sworn to protect. This was his home, the place where he had built his life and raised his family. But now the heavens themselves seemed to threaten everything he held dear.

"Father, will you teach me the Call of the Tempest today?"

An eager voice pulled him from his thoughts. He turned around to find his daughter, Elara, her dark curls dancing in the wind as she bounded up to him, her green eyes sparkling in anticipation. Zephyros smiled, though his heart was heavy.

"Not today, little storm. Your mother will have my head if I keep you out here too late."

With her arms crossed, Elara pouted, "You always say that! How will I ever become stronger than you if you never teach me?"

A soft laugh echoed from behind them. "She has a point, you know." Lyra, his wife, carrying their youngest, a boy of three winters named Caelum, was gliding behind him as if a gentle breeze was holding her up. "You were already a master of the skies at her age."

Zephyros walked over and placed a gentle kiss on Lyra's forehead. "And you were already winning every heart with your charms, including mine."

Lyra smiled, but there was a shadow in her eyes. "Zephyros, have you noticed anything…strange lately? The winds feel different, as if something is coming."

His gaze turned back to the horizon, his heart tightening with an unnamed dread. "I have felt it too," he admitted. "The skies whisper of a storm greater than any we've known."

Before they could continue, the air suddenly grew still, the very winds that Zephyros commanded seeming to hold their breath. The clouds above swirled unnaturally, darkening with a rapidity that sent a chill down his spine.

"Zephyros…" Lyra squeaked, her grip tightening on Caelum.

And then the sky tore open. A blinding light surged through the heavens, and from it descended a figure wreathed in golden flames, wings of light spreading wide. It was Solara, the Radiant, Goddess of the Sun, her face cold and unforgiving.

"Zephyros, Stormcaller of Aetheros," her voice boomed across the valley, "you have defied the natural order, wielding powers beyond your mortal station. The gods have decreed that your line shall end."

Elara clung to her father's robes, her earlier bravado replaced by terror.

"Father, what's happening?"

"Stay close, Elara," Zephyros whispered, his heart pounding. He turned to face the goddess, his hand tightening around his staff. "Solara, my powers are a gift, given to protect my people! What right do you have to take that from me?"

Another figure descended beside Solara, this one cloaked in shadows, with eyes like the Abyss—Umbra, the Veiled, Goddess of Night. "Your arrogance has led you to believe you are above the gods, Zephyros," she said, her voice a chilling whisper. "And now, you and your kin shall pay the price."

"No!" Zephyros roared, raising his staff to the sky. Lightning crackled in the darkened clouds, but as he summoned his might, he realized with growing horror that the storm would not answer. The skies had betrayed him, bowing to the will of the gods.

In a desperate act, Zephyros turned to his wife. "Lyra, take the children! Get them to safety!"

But it was too late. With a gesture from Solara, a beam of searing light shot toward them. Zephyros threw himself in front of his family, casting a shield of wind and lightning, but the divine power was too great. The shield shattered, and the light consumed them. When the brilliance faded, Zephyros collapsed on the scorched earth, his body broken. He struggled to rise, his vision blurred by pain and loss. He reached out, trembling, to where his family had been.

But they were gone. Only ashes remained.

A laugh echoed from the skies, and Zephyros looked up to see Solara and Umbra, their expressions indifferent. "Let this be a lesson to all who defy the gods," Solara declared before the two deities vanished into the sky, leaving only silence and the smell of burning earth.

Zephyros crawled to the place where Lyra had stood, his fingers sifting through the ash. Tears streamed down his face, mixing with the blood on his lips. "I will not let this stand," he whispered, his voice hoarse and broken. "You will pay for this…all of you."

The wind began to howl again, answering his rage. The sky, once his ally, now wept with him. In the distance, the mountain peaks of Aetheros loomed, their shadows growing longer as night fell. And as the stars began to blink into existence, a new determination filled Zephyros's heart.

Returning home, he sat in his study, the dim light of a single candle flickering against the ancient stone walls. The room was filled with the relics of his past: tomes of forgotten knowledge, artifacts from distant lands, and a globe of Aetheros that had once fascinated his daughter. Now, it was all but meaningless. His hands trembled as he reached out to the small wooden carving on his desk, a simple figure of a bird that Elara had made. He clutched it tightly, his knuckles white, as he fought back the waves of grief that threatened to consume him.

The wind outside howled mournfully, as if sharing in his sorrow. He closed his eyes, and for a moment he could almost hear Lyra's laughter, see Elara's bright smile, feel Caelum's small hand in his. But the memories only sharpened the pain, a constant reminder of all he had lost. A soft knock on the door broke through the silence.

Zephyros didn't look up, his voice rough and hollow. "Leave me."

The door creaked open anyway, and he heard the shuffling of boots on the stone floor. "Forgive me, Zephyros," a deep, yet gentle voice spoke, "but I could not stay away."

Zephyros finally looked up, his eyes bloodshot and weary. Standing before him was a dwarf, not tall but broad and sturdy, with a long, mossy-green beard that seemed to flow like the very earth he commanded. His robes were the color of rich soil, and woven into them were vines and leaves that seemed to pulse with life. This was Thrain, the Verdant Sage, a wizard whose connection to the natural world was unmatched, and one of the few who Zephyros considered a true friend.

"Thrain…" Zephyros's voice broke, and he turned away, unable to meet the dwarf's compassionate gaze.

Thrain stepped closer, his presence as calming as a forest glade. "I heard the winds," he said softly. "They carried your sorrow to me. I know what happened."

Zephyros clenched his fists, his anger flaring briefly. "Then you know that they are gone. My family…reduced to ashes by those cursed gods."

Thrain nodded, his expression somber. "I do. And I am truly sorry, my friend. No words can mend the pain you feel." Silence hung between them, heavy with the weight of loss. Thrain finally broke it, his voice quiet but firm. "Zephyros, I have known you for many years. You are not one to bow before the gods, even in the face of such tragedy. And I can see it in your eyes. Revenge burns within you."

Zephyros looked at Thrain, his eyes cold and distant. "Revenge? It's all I have left. But what can I do? The gods are beyond my reach, and my power alone is not enough."

Thrain's gaze grew more intense. "There may be a way, though it is fraught with peril. I have heard whispers of a being—an assassin whose very name strikes fear into the hearts of the divine. He is said to be one with the storms, with the clouds and lightning at his command, as you are."

Zephyros frowned, his interest piqued despite his grief. "An assassin strong enough to kill a god?"

"Yes," Thrain replied, "they say he can strike down even the mightiest of beings, leaving no trace of his presence. But his last-known sighting was in a place where few dare to tread—a realm shrouded in darkness and despair, where the very air is thick with the whispers of the damned."

Zephyros leaned forward, his eyes narrowing. "You speak of the Abyssal Depths, the land where souls are lost and hope is but a distant memory."

Thrain nodded solemnly. "It is a place where only the most desperate venture, for it is said that those who enter never return. But if you seek this assassin, Kumori, that is where you must go." Zephyros was silent for a long moment, the weight of Thrain's words settling over him like a heavy cloak. The Abyssal Depths were a place so feared that even the gods rarely spoke of it. And yet if this Kumori could truly help him avenge his family, then he had no choice.

"Thrain," Zephyros finally said, his voice resolute, "I must find this assassin. If he is my only hope of bringing the gods to their knees, then I will go, no matter the cost."

The Verdant Sage placed a hand on Zephyros's shoulder, his grip firm and reassuring.

"I feared you would say that. Just know, my friend, that you do not have to face this alone. There are those who still stand with you."

Zephyros nodded, though his heart remained heavy. "Thank you. Your support means more to me than you know. But this path... It is one I must walk alone."

Thrain's eyes softened, and he nodded in understanding. "Very well. But remember, the earth and the sky are still with you, even in the darkest of places." He turned and left the study, his footsteps echoing in the empty halls. Zephyros watched him go, his mind already turning to the journey ahead.

The Abyssal Depths, where souls were lost and only the most desperate would dare to tread. If that was where he would find Kumori, then that was where he would go. And so, the Stormcaller of Aetheros, the man who once danced with the winds, began his descent into darkness, his heart set on revenge, his mind on the assassin known only as Kumori.

CHAPTER 2

Night in the Shadowed Vale was like no other, a perfect shroud of darkness where the light of the stars barely pierced the dense canopy of trees. The air was thick with the scent of moss and earth, the sounds of nocturnal creatures echoing in the distance. This was the land of the Dark Elves, a hidden sanctuary where the shadows themselves were alive and where the art of assassination was not just a skill, but a way of life.

In the heart of the Vale, beneath the twisted roots of an ancient tree that towered above the rest, a group of young elves trained in silence. Their movements were precise, deadly, each strike meant to kill. Among them, a figure moved with unmatched grace and speed, his presence like a wisp of shadow in the night.

Kumori was slender yet muscular, his skin a deep shade of onyx, almost blending into the darkness around him. His eyes, sharp and gleaming like silver, were the only thing that caught the scarce light, reflecting a cold determination. His long, white hair was pulled back tightly, falling in a single braid down his back. Twin daggers, their blades etched with ancient runes, were strapped to his thighs, and the air around him crackled faintly with the energy of a storm that was always just beneath the surface.

As he finished a series of complex maneuvers, he turned to his companion, a young elf with skin like rich soil and hair the color of dark clay. Iwamaru was Kumori's closest friend and one of the few who could match his skill. Where Kumori was the storm, Iwamaru was the earth—solid, unyielding, and deadly in his own way. His eyes were a deep green, reflecting the strength and patience of the forests from which he drew his power.

"You're getting faster," Iwamaru remarked, a rare smile tugging at his lips as he watched Kumori finish his routine.

Kumori wiped the sweat from his brow, his expression as unreadable as always. "And you're getting stronger. Soon we'll have no rivals left in the Vale."

Iwamaru chuckled, a low, rumbling sound. "Maybe, but strength isn't everything. The elders say that our greatest test is yet to come."

Kumori's gaze darkened, his thoughts drifting to the harsh training they had endured since childhood. The Vale was not just a place of training; it was a crucible, where only the strongest survived.

"Do you think we're ready, Iwa? For whatever it is?"

"I don't know, but I do know this. Whatever comes, we face it together."

Kumori nodded, his resolve hardening. Iwamaru was more than a friend; he was a brother in arms, someone who understood the burden of their shared fate. They had been trained to be killers, to become shadows in the night, and yet there was always the nagging thought of what was beyond the Vale. The elders spoke in hushed tones of missions that no one returned from, of enemies that were not mortal.

His friend's rough voice broke through his thoughts. "Do you ever wonder if there's more to this? More than training, more than killing?"

Silver eyes met green. "I used to. But now I think it's all there is. We were born for this, trained for this. What else could there be?"

Iwamaru looked up at the dark sky, his eyes thoughtful. "I don't know. But sometimes I feel like there's something…bigger out there. Something 'they're not telling us."

Before Kumori could respond, a figure emerged from the shadows—a tall elf with a presence that commanded silence. It was Elder Varun, one of the leaders of the Dark Elves, a master assassin whose very name was spoken with reverence and fear. Varun's voice was deep and resonant, like the distant rumble of thunder.

"Boys, your training here is complete."

The two young elves exchanged a glance, their hearts quickening. This was the moment they had been waiting for, the moment that would define their lives.

"The time has come for you to leave the Vale," Varun continued, his eyes cold and calculating. "You will face trials unlike any you have known. And if you survive, you will earn your place among the shadows."

Iwamaru clenched his fists, his determination clear. "We are ready, Elder."

Varun's gaze shifted to Kumori, as if weighing his very soul. "And you, Kumori? Are you prepared to embrace the storm within you, to become the weapon you were born to be?"

Kumori felt the crackle of lightning beneath his skin, the power that had always been a part of him. He met Varun's gaze without flinching. "I am ready." Varun nodded, satisfied.

"Good. Then prepare yourselves. Tomorrow, you begin your first mission. And know this—if you succeed, even the gods will fear you."

As the elder slipped silently into the shadows, the two friends stood in silence, the weight of what was ahead pressing down on them. The Vale, the only home they had ever known, was now behind them. Before them was a path shrouded in mystery, where their skills would be tested beyond anything they could imagine.

"I guess this is it," Iwamaru said quietly, his voice tinged with both excitement and trepidation. Kumori nodded, his expression unreadable.

"Yes, this is where it all begins." And with that, the two young assassins stood side by side, ready to face whatever destiny had in store for them.

* * *

The town of Valandor was a place of ethereal beauty, nestled high in the emerald hills that overlooked the Valley of Aetheros. The streets were paved with smooth, white stone that shimmered in the sunlight. Buildings, tall and graceful, were adorned with intricate carvings of vines and flowers that seemed to grow from the very walls. Tall spires reached toward the sky, their tips gleaming with golden light, while the air was filled with the scent of blooming jasmine and the soft melodies of the wind chimes that hung from every archway.

As Zephyros guided his cart through the bustling town square, he could not help but feel a pang of sorrow. Valandor had once been a place of joy for him, a place where he and Lyra had spent many happy days together. Now, the beauty of the town only deepened his sense of loss.

The cart was nearly ready, laden with supplies for the journey ahead. Three majestic horses, their coats shimmering like polished obsidian, were hitched to the cart, their breaths forming clouds in the cool morning air. Zephyros moved with purpose, though his movements were stiff, as if weighed down by an invisible burden.

As he secured the last of the provisions, a voice, gentle yet filled with a quiet power, reached his ears. "Zephyros."

He turned to see a figure standing a few paces away, a tall Altmer clad in robes of pure white that seemed to glow with an inner light. His long, golden hair cascaded over his shoulders, and his eyes, a piercing blue, held a calm intensity. This was Elion, Lyra's brother, a mage of great renown, known not only for his mastery of light magic but for the fear he instilled in those who opposed him.

"Elion," Zephyros acknowledged, his voice steady but lacking warmth, "I did not expect to see you here."

The Altmer stepped closer, his gaze unwavering.

"I heard of what happened and came as soon as I could."

Zephyros turned away, tightening the straps on the cart. "There's nothing you can do. What's done is done."

Elion's expression softened, though there was a steeliness behind his eyes. "Perhaps, but that does not mean you should face this alone." Zephyros stiffened, his hands pausing in their work.

"This is my fight, Elion. My family… Lyra… They're gone because of me. The gods will pay, but this is my burden and no one else's."

"And do you think Lyra would want you to do this alone?" Elion appeared determined. "She was my sister. Do not think for a moment that I do not share in your grief, in your desire for vengeance. But I also know that she would not want you to lose yourself in that darkness."

Zephyros said nothing, his jaw clenched as he fought the surge of emotion threatening to overwhelm him. Before the silence could stretch too long, a merchant, a sprightly high elf with a bright smile and keen eyes, approached them.

"Master Zephyros!" he called out, sounding cheerful. "Heading out on a journey, I see. Anything else you might need before you go? Perhaps some enchanted arrows? A cloak woven with spells of protection?"

Zephyros forced a small, tight-lipped smile. "I have all that I need, Varnen. Thank you."

The merchant nodded, though his eyes lingered on the two figures, sensing the tension between them. "Very well, then. Safe travels, my friend. And if you find yourself needing anything, you know where to find me." With a polite bow, Varnen retreated to his stall, leaving Zephyros and Elion alone once more.

Elion watched as Zephyros continued his preparations, his movements more deliberate now. "Zephyros, I am not here to take over your mission but let me help you. The path you are about to walk is treacherous, and the enemies you seek are beyond even your considerable power."

Zephyros turned to face Elion, his eyes burning with a mixture of anger and despair. "And what would you have me do? Wait? Hope that the gods show mercy? No, Elion. They took everything from me, and I will see them fall, even if it costs me my life."

Elion did not flinch at Zephyros's outburst. Instead, he stepped closer, his voice calm but firm. "Then let me help you see it through. Lyra may be gone, but you are still here. And as long as you are, I will not let you face this alone."

Zephyros met Elion's gaze, the resolve in those blue eyes mirroring his own. For a long moment, they stood in silence, the tension between them palpable. But slowly the anger in Zephyros's eyes softened, replaced by a deep, aching sadness.

"Very well," he finally said, his voice heavy. "You can come. But I will not be swayed from my path, no matter what happens."

Elion nodded. "I would expect nothing less."

As the two men finished preparing the cart, the sun began to rise higher in the sky, casting shadows over the town of Valandor. The time for mourning was over. Now it was the time for action.

CHAPTER 3

Shadowed Vale was alive with the sound of crickets and the gentle rustling of leaves. Kumori and Iwa progressed through the narrow, winding streets of the small town nestled within the Vale, the faint glow of lanterns illuminating their path. The town was a quiet, secluded place, home to their tribe of dark elves, where the shadows were deep, and the nights were long.

Tonight, they'd decided to indulge in a rare moment of relaxation. They headed toward the Gloaming Lantern, the local pub that served as a gathering place for warriors, hunters, and those who sought solace in the company of others. The pub was a modest building, its stone walls covered in ivy and its wooden beams worn smooth by time. Inside, the warm glow of the hearth welcomed them, along with the scent of roasting meat and freshly baked bread.

The two friends took a seat at a corner table, away from the prying eyes of the other patrons. The air was thick with the sounds of laughter, clinking mugs, and the soft strumming of a lute played by a bard in another corner. A serving girl approached them, her smile bright despite the late hour.

"What'll it be tonight, lads?" she asked, her voice cheerful.

"Two plates of whatever's fresh, and a pitcher of your strongest ale," Iwa replied with a grin.

Kumori nodded in agreement, leaning back in his chair as he surveyed the room. It wasn't often they had the chance to relax like this, and he intended to savor it.

As their food arrived, steaming and fragrant, they dug in with gusto, the stress of their training and the weight of their future momentarily forgotten.

After a while, Iwa broke the comfortable silence. "Have you ever thought about what you really want out of all this?"

Kumori looked up from his plate, his silver eyes thoughtful. "What do you mean?"

"I mean, this life we've been training for—the missions, the trials, the killing. What's your end goal?"

Iwa leaned forward, his green eyes serious. "For me, I've always wanted to get stronger, to prove myself. I want to take over for Varun someday, lead our tribe, protect our people. But you… You're different."

Kumori considered that, the flickering firelight casting shadows across his face. "Adventure," he finally said. "I want to see the world, experience things beyond the Vale. We've been trained to survive, to fight, but what's the point if we never leave these shadows? I want to test myself, not only against other warriors, but against the world itself."

Iwa chuckled, shaking his head. "I should have known. You've always had that restless spirit. But the world outside isn't like the Vale. It's dangerous, unpredictable."

"So is this place," Kumori countered. "But that's what makes it worth it. Don't you ever wonder what's out there, beyond these hills?"

Iwa shrugged. "Sometimes, but my place is here. I have responsibilities to our tribe, to our people. Someday, I'll be the one making the decisions, guiding our warriors. That's my path."

Kumori smiled faintly. "And I'll be out there, finding new challenges, new battles. But no matter where I go, this place will always be home."

Iwa raised his mug in a toast. "To the future then, whatever it holds."

Kumori clinked his mug against Iwa's, the sound of their laughter mingling with the noise of the pub. For tonight, they were merely two friends enjoying a rare moment of peace. But tomorrow, the pressure of their destiny would return, and they would be ready to face it.

The next morning, Kumori and Iwa continued to the heart of the Shadowed Vale, where the ancient tree that housed the council of elders stood. Its massive roots twisted and turned, forming natural pathways and chambers within the earth. The air here was thick with the scent of moss and damp wood, and the whispers of the elders echoed through the hollow spaces.

Varun, the leader of their tribe and a master assassin, awaited them in one of the secluded chambers. His presence was as imposing as ever, his eyes sharp and calculating. He wasted no time with pleasantries.

Varun's voice was low and measured. "Your training has been completed. It is time for your first real mission."

The two young assassins listened intently, their earlier light-heartedness replaced by focused determination.

"There is a task that requires your skills," Varun continued. "In the capital of Elarion, the emperor's son must be eliminated."

Iwa's brow furrowed slightly. "The emperor's son? Why him?"

Varun's expression darkened. "The emperor is a tyrant, but he is not the true threat. He is being controlled and manipulated by a darker force from the Abyssal Depths. His son, however, has shown signs of resistance, of breaking free from this influence. He is a threat to the balance we maintain."

Kumori's eyes narrowed. "So we are to prevent this by eliminating him?"

"Yes," Varun replied. "But be warned, the capital is heavily guarded, and the emperor's son is no fool. He will not be easily taken. This mission will test your skills and your resolve."

Kumori and Iwa nodded, accepting the gravity of the task. They knew this was more than a mission—it was a trial that would define their futures as assassins.

As they left the chamber, the weight of their assignment settled over them. There would be no turning back now.

*　*　*

The bustling capital of Elarion was alive with activity, its streets filled with merchants, soldiers, and citizens going about their daily lives. The capital was a place of grandeur and opulence, its buildings tall and majestic, with walls adorned by tapestries and statues of past emperors.

At the heart of the city stood the imperial palace, a towering structure of white marble and gold. Its spires reached toward the sky, and its halls were lined with columns of polished stone. The palace was a symbol of the emperor's power, but within its walls, something darker stirred.

The emperor, a man of once-great stature, now sat on his throne, his eyes vacant and his mind clouded. Beside him, his wife, the empress, looked on with a mixture of concern and fear. Their son, Prince Aethas, stood nearby, his expression troubled as he watched his father's slow descent into madness.

Aethas approached his mother, his voice low. "Mother, something is wrong with Father. He is not himself."

The empress nodded, her eyes filled with sorrow. "I know, my son, but there is nothing we can do. Whatever darkness has taken hold of him is beyond our power to relieve."

Aethas clenched his fists, his resolve hardening. "I will not let this continue. I will find a way to free him, even if it means going against everything I've been taught."

As Aethas left the throne room, a shadowed figure lingered in one corner, watching with cold, calculating eyes. It was the being from the Abyssal Depths, its presence hidden from all but those it wished to control. The emperor was merely a puppet, his strings pulled by something far more sinister.

As day turned to night, the capital continued to bustle with life, unaware of the darkness that threatened to consume it from within. And in the shadows, two assassins prepared to carry out their mission.

The air between them was thick with unspoken resolve as they turned toward the horizon, unaware of the threads of fate that had already weaving around them. Above, the pale moon bathed the capital in its silver glow, another quiet night settled in. For now, all was still.

CHAPTER 4

The sun was high in the sky as Kumori and Iwa approached the gates of Elarion, the capital city, their hoods drawn low to shield their faces from the guards' scrutiny. The city loomed before them, its white walls gleaming in the daylight, a stark contrast to the dark mission they had come to fulfill.

The gates were massive, made of iron and wood reinforced with steel bands. Guards in gleaming armor stood at attention, their eyes sharp as they watched the steady stream of travelers, merchants, and citizens entering the city. The two assassins had taken on the guise of simple travelers—Kumori as a merchant, with a cart of wares covered in a cloth, and Iwa as his bodyguard, a common enough sight in the bustling capital.

"Remember," Kumori murmured to Iwa as they approached the guards, "We're simply passing through. Act natural."

Iwa gave a slight nod, his face impassive. "I know the drill."

As they reached the gates, one of the guards stepped forward, his hand raised. "Halt! State your business in Elarion."

Kumori adopted a friendly smile, his voice light and unassuming. "Good day, sir. We're merchants from the west, here to sell our wares in the city market. We've heard great things about Elarion and wanted to see it for ourselves."

The guard eyed them for a moment, his gaze flicking between the cart and the two men. After a tense pause, he nodded. "Very well. You may enter, but be mindful of the curfew. No one is allowed in the streets after dark."

"Of course, sir. We'll be sure to follow the rules," Kumori replied with a respectful nod.

The guards stepped aside, allowing them to pass through the gates and into the city.

Once inside, Kumori and Iwa allowed themselves a moment to take in their surroundings. Elarion was a city of grandeur, its streets wide and paved with smooth stone, the buildings towering and majestic. Banners in the colors of the empire, crimson and gold, fluttered from every corner, and the air was filled with the scents of exotic spices, roasting meats, and freshly baked bread.

The city was alive with activity, merchants peddling their goods, children playing in the streets, and nobles riding in carriages, their fine clothes and jewelry sparkling in the sunlight. It was a world away from the Shadowed Vale they called home, a place where the darkness was hidden beneath layers of wealth and power.

"We need to find a place to wait until nightfall," Kumori said quietly, his eyes scanning the streets for potential vantage points. "Somewhere close to the palace but out of sight."

Iwa nodded; his expression thoughtful. They traversed the city, marveling at the beauty and how magnificent it was. "There's an inn near the market district. It's busy enough that we won't stand out, but it's close to the palace gates. We can keep watch from there."

They continued through the winding streets, moving with the practiced ease of those who knew how to blend into any environment. The inn Iwa had mentioned was a modest establishment, its wooden sign swinging gently in the breeze. The sound of laughter and clinking mugs drifted from inside, mingling with the warm, comforting scent of ale and stew.

After securing a room, they spent the rest of the day scouting the city, familiarizing themselves with the layout and identifying potential entry points into the palace. The streets were patrolled by guards, but the palace itself was the true fortress, its high walls and numerous watchtowers a testament to the emperor's paranoia.

As the sun began to set, they returned to the inn, their plan in place. They would wait until the cover of night before making their move, slipping into the palace unseen and completing their mission before anyone realized what had happened.

* * *

In another part of the city, Prince Aethas was making his own preparations. He moved through the crowded streets with purpose, his cloak drawn tightly around him to avoid recognition. Aethas had spent the past weeks searching for answers, seeking out any information that might help him free his father from the dark influence that had taken hold of him.

He'd heard whispers of an organization that operated in the shadows, a group of skilled warriors and mages who specialized in dealing with the supernatural. If anyone could help him, it would be them. But finding them had proven more difficult than he anticipated.

As he passed through the market district, Aethas paused in front of a small, plain shop tucked away in a narrow alley. The sign above the door was faded, the lettering barely visible, but he knew this was the place he had been searching for.

Taking a deep breath, Aethas pushed open the door and stepped inside. The interior was dimly lit, the air thick with the scent of incense and old parchment. Shelves lined the walls, filled with books, scrolls, and various arcane artifacts. Behind the counter stood an old man, his eyes sharp despite his age.

"Welcome," the man said in a raspy voice. "What brings you to my humble shop, young prince?"

Aethas stiffened at the recognition but kept his composure. "I need information. I've heard rumors of a group that deals with…unusual matters. I'm looking for them."

The old man studied him for a moment then nodded slowly. "You seek the Circle of Shadows. They are not easy to find and even harder to trust. But if you are determined, I may be able to point you in the right direction."

Aethas's heart quickened with hope. "Please, I'll do whatever it takes."

The man smiled faintly. "Be careful what you wish for, young prince. The shadows are not as forgiving as the light." He handed Aethas a small, folded piece of parchment. "This will lead you to them. Remember, they are not your friends, and their help comes at a price."

Aethas took the parchment, his mind racing with possibilities. "Thank you. I won't forget this."

As he left the shop, Aethas couldn't shake the feeling that he was stepping into something far more dangerous than he had anticipated. But he had no choice. His father's life and the fate of the empire depended on him.

* * *

Back at the inn, night had fallen, and the city was enveloped by darkness. Kumori and Iwa stood at the window of their room, watching the palace from afar.

"It's time," Kumori said, his voice low and steady. "Let's go."

They slipped out of the inn, their forms melting into the shadows as they crept toward the palace. The streets were quiet now, the curfew keeping most of the city's inhabitants indoors. The guards at the palace gates were alert but never saw the two figures who passed silently by them, slipping through the hidden passage they had discovered earlier.

As they approached the palace walls, Kumori and Iwa paused, their senses heightened as they prepared for the task ahead. The moonlight glinted off the polished stone, casting eerie shadows that danced in the night.

The castle loomed before them, its towering spires reaching into the sky like the talons of some great beast. They had come to fulfill their mission, but Kumori couldn't shake the feeling that something far greater was at play.

"Ready?" Iwa asked, his voice barely a whisper.

Kumori nodded, his eyes narrowing with determination. "Let's do this."

With the cover of darkness cloaking their movements, they began their infiltration. Sticking to the shadows, Kumori and Iwa scaled the outer walls with the ease of seasoned assassins, their hands finding every crevice and ledge worn smooth by time. Once at the top, they crouched low, their eyes scanning the palace grounds. The guards patrolled in a steady rhythm, but the pair moved in perfect sync, darting across the rooftops like whispers on the wind.

Reaching a narrow balcony that overlooked a less guarded wing, Kumori deftly picked the lock on a side door, slipping inside the emperor's domain. They moved through the dimly lit corridors with silent precision, their senses sharp, completely unaware that, even now, events were unfolding beyond their control—events that would soon alter the course of their lives forever.

CHAPTER 5

Aethas slipped back into his chambers, his heart still racing from the encounter in the old shop. The parchment felt heavy in his hand, a tangible reminder of the path he was about to take. He lit a small candle on his desk, its flickering light casting shadows on the walls as he unfolded the parchment. The writing was delicate, almost ethereal, with symbols and directions that seemed to shift as he read them.

"This is it," he whispered to himself, his voice filled with a mix of determination and uncertainty. He knew that if he were to free his father from the dark influence that had taken hold of him, he would need help from forces beyond the palace walls. The Circle of Shadows might be his only hope, but their reputation made him wary.

As he studied the parchment, tracing the symbols with his finger, a sense of foreboding washed over him.

The candlelight flickered, and for a moment he thought he saw movement in the shadows. But when he looked up, the room was still, the only sound the crackling of the fire in the hearth.

Meanwhile, Kumori and Iwa moved like wraiths through the darkened corridors of the palace. They had managed to bypass the outer guards and were now deep within the heart of the emperor's stronghold. The walls were lined with tapestries depicting scenes of conquest and power, but the grandeur of the surroundings did nothing to ease the tension that hung between them.

As they rounded a corner, Kumori held up a hand, signaling Iwa to stop. Ahead of them, in the dim light of the corridor, they saw the emperor. He was pacing slowly, his head bowed as if deep in thought. But there was something wrong. His movements were stiff, almost mechanical, and his eyes, once bright with intelligence, were now dull and vacant.

Iwa leaned in close, his voice barely a whisper. "He looks like a puppet…like someone else is pulling the strings."

Kumori nodded, his eyes narrowing as he watched the emperor's every move. "Something has taken control of him. This mission is more complicated than we thought."

Before they could ponder further, they heard the soft rustle of fabric and the faint sound of footsteps approaching from the other end of the corridor. They melted back into the shadows, their breathing controlled, as they observed the new arrivals.

The queen, resplendent in a deep-crimson gown, walked with purpose, her expression cold and calculating. But it was the figure beside her that caught Kumori's attention. The man was tall and imposing, draped in a dark cloak that seemed to absorb the light around him. His eyes glowed with a malevolent purple hue, casting an eerie glow on his gaunt, pale face. There was an air of power about him, a dark energy that made the hairs on the back of Kumori's neck stand on end.

As the queen and the wizard passed, Kumori and Iwa strained to hear their conversation.

"Everything is proceeding as planned," the queen murmured with an unsettling confidence. "My husband is completely under our control, thanks to your master's power."

The wizard's voice was cold, almost inhuman. "The creature from the Abyss demands results. The emperor's son is the last obstacle. Once he is dealt with, the throne will belong to us entirely."

The queen's lips curled into a cruel smile. "He won't be a problem. Soon, he will be gone, and the empire will be ours to rule."

As they moved out of earshot, Kumori and Iwa exchanged a grim look. The queen was a traitor, conspiring with forces from the Abyss to control the emperor and seize power. Their mission had reached a new level of danger.

"We need to find the prince," Kumori whispered. "Now."

They moved swiftly but cautiously through the palace, their senses heightened. The corridors were a maze of opulence and confusion, but they had studied the layout well. Finally, they reached the door to Aethas's chambers.

Kumori signaled for Iwa to stay back as he approached the door. He could hear the faint sound of pages turning, the prince deep in his studies. Taking a deep breath, Kumori pushed the door open and slipped inside.

Aethas looked up from the parchment, his eyes widening in surprise as he saw the two figures in his doorway. But he didn't hesitate. With a swift motion, he cast the parchment aside and reached for the sword at his side, drawing it with a sharp hiss of steel.

"You picked the wrong room," Aethas said, his voice steady despite the tension in the air.

Kumori didn't respond. Instead, he moved forward, his daggers gleaming in the dim light. But Aethas was quick, his sword flashing as he parried Kumori's first strike. The two clashed in a flurry of motion, the sound of metal-on-metal ringing through the chamber.

Iwa moved to flank Aethas, but the prince was no ordinary opponent. He shifted his stance, sending a wave of energy toward Iwa with a flick of his hand. The magic hit like a hammer, forcing Iwa to step back, his eyes narrowing in surprise.

"You have magic," Kumori remarked, dodging another of Aethas's strikes.

"And I know how to use it," Aethas shot back, sending a bolt of lightning toward Kumori, whose body twisted out of the way with practiced ease.

For a moment, it seemed as though the fight would continue, but Kumori did something unexpected. He sheathed his daggers and held up his hands in a gesture of peace.

"Wait," Kumori said, "We're not here to kill you."

Aethas hesitated, his sword still raised, but he didn't strike. "Then what do you want?"

"To talk," Iwa said, stepping forward, his posture relaxed but ready. "We know what's going on in this palace. We know about your father's illness and the queen's betrayal. We can help you."

Aethas's eyes flickered with uncertainty. "Why should I trust you? You are assassins, aren't you?"

"We were sent to kill you," Kumori admitted candidly, "but things have changed. We overheard the queen and her…associate. There's a greater threat at play here, something from the Abyss. We're not your enemies. We want to stop this as much as you do."

Aethas lowered his sword slightly, the tension in his shoulders easing. "And how do you propose to do that?"

"Come with us," Iwa said. "We can take you to our leader, Varun. He's dealt with dark forces before. If anyone can help free your father and stop the queen, it's him."

Aethas studied them for a long moment, the weight of his decision clear in his eyes. Finally, he nodded, sheathing his sword. "Very well. I'll go with you, but I'll be watching you closely. If you betray me…"

"We won't," Kumori said with a grin. "You have my word."

With an agreement reached, the three of them began making their preparations to leave the palace. The night was still dark, the shadows deep. They slipped out into the courtyard, moving swiftly and silently.

As they left the castle behind, the weight of what was ahead settled over them. The Shadowed Vale awaited, and perhaps the answers they all sought.

A new alliance had been forged in the shadows.

CHAPTER 6

The morning sun was beginning to crest over the horizon as Zephyros and Elion made their final preparations to leave the high elven town of Valandor. The town was still, its streets quiet in the early-dawn light, but the weight of their journey ahead pressed heavily on their minds.

Zephyros was securing the last of their supplies to the cart, his thoughts already focused on the road ahead. Elion, meanwhile, was silently going over the map they had acquired, tracing their path toward the Shadowed Vale. The journey would be long and fraught with danger, but both men were resolute in their mission.

As they were about to set off, a silky voice called out from behind them. "Elion, wait!"

Elion turned, his heart clenching as he saw his wife, Selene, running toward them, their infant daughter cradled in her arms. Selene was a vision of grace, her long golden hair flowing in the morning breeze, her eyes a deep, calming blue that held both sorrow and strength. She was the embodiment of serenity, yet there was a deep sadness etched into her features.

"Selene…" Elion breathed, his voice filled with both love and pain.

Selene reached him, her breath coming in soft gasps from the exertion, but she managed a smile, one that was bittersweet. "I knew you would leave without saying goodbye," she said, her voice trembling slightly, though she quickly steadied herself.

Elion's heart ached as he looked at her, at the woman he had loved for so long, who had stood by him through every trial. He gently placed a hand on her cheek, his thumb brushing away a tear that had escaped.

"I didn't want to make it harder for you," he said softly. "For us."

Selene shook her head, her eyes searching his. "It's already hard, Elion, but I understand. You have a duty, and I knew this day would come." She paused, her gaze dropping to their daughter, who was sleeping peacefully in her arms. "But that doesn't make it any easier."

Elion leaned forward, pressing his forehead against hers, their breaths mingling as they stood there, savoring the closeness. "You and Lyra are my heart, Selene. Leaving you is the hardest thing I've ever had to do."

Selene closed her eyes, taking solace in his voice. "And we will be here when you return. I'll keep the hearth warm, and I'll take care of our daughter. We'll be waiting for you, Elion, no matter how long it takes."

Elion gave her a kiss filled with all the love, longing, and fear he couldn't put into words. It was a kiss that spoke of promises, of hope, and of a future they would fight to see.

When they finally pulled apart, Selene smiled through her tears. "Be safe," she whispered. "Come back to us."

Elion nodded, his own eyes glistening with unshed tears. "I will. I swear it."

With one last lingering touch, Elion turned and gently took his daughter from Selene's arms, holding her close for a moment. The baby stirred, her tiny hand clutching at his robe, and Elion's heart broke all over again.

"Goodbye, little one," he whispered, kissing her forehead before handing her back to Selene.

As he stepped back, Selene reached out and caught his hand, squeezing it tightly. "We'll be here," she repeated, her voice strong despite the tears. "Always."

Elion squeezed her hand in return, a silent promise passing between them before he finally released her and turned to Zephyros, who had watched the exchange in respectful silence.

"It's time," Elion said, his voice steady once more.

Zephyros nodded, giving Selene a small, respectful bow before he took the reins of the cart. "Let's go."

As they began to leave, Selene watched them, standing tall and strong, holding her daughter close. She didn't move until they were out of sight, and even then she didn't cry. She had to be strong—for herself, for her daughter, and for the man she loved.

The road ahead was long, and Selene knew it would be filled with danger. But she also knew that Elion would do everything in his power to return to them. And so, with a heart full of love and hope, she turned back toward their home, ready to wait as long as it took.

The journey away from Valandor was quiet, the only sound the steady clop of hooves and the creak of the cart's wheels. Elion kept his eyes forward, though his thoughts were still with his wife and daughter, the memory of their farewell playing over in his mind.

Zephyros, sensing his friend's turmoil, remained silent, giving him the space he needed. He knew the weight of leaving loved ones behind, the pain of knowing you might never see them again. But he also knew that Elion was strong and that his love for his family would only fuel his resolve.

After several hours of travel, they reached the outskirts of Valandor, the familiar rolling hills giving way to denser forests and rougher terrain. The map they carried showed the general direction of the Shadowed Vale, but the exact location was hidden, known only to those who had been there before.

As the sun began to dip low in the sky, they approached a small town nestled in a valley between two hills. The town was unremarkable, its buildings simple and its streets quiet, but it was a known stop for travelers heading into more dangerous lands. If there was anyone who could point them toward the Shadowed Vale, it would be here.

They made their way to the town's center, where a modest inn stood, its wooden sign creaking gently in the evening breeze. The inn's name, The Wanderer's Rest, was painted in faded letters above the door. It looked like the kind of place where rumors and secrets were traded over mugs of ale, where those seeking knowledge might find what they were looking for.

After securing a room and some food, Zephyros and Elion settled into a corner of the common room, their eyes scanning the other patrons. The inn was lively enough, with a mix of travelers, merchants, and locals filling the space, but they needed someone with knowledge of the Shadowed Vale.

The meal began with a warm loaf of rustic bread, freshly baked and served with herb-infused butter. As the main course, they'd enjoy a platter of roasted venison, slow-cooked to perfection with a rich, dark gravy made from wild mushrooms and red wine. On the side, a medley of roasted root vegetables—carrots, parsnips, and potatoes—seasoned with rosemary and garlic.

To complement the savory flavors, a side dish of spiced rice, fragrant with cinnamon and cloves, balanced the richness of the meal. They finished with a local specialty: honeyed figs and goat cheese, drizzled with a touch of lavender syrup, offering a sweet yet subtle end to the feast. All of this washed down with a flagon of Wanderer's Mead, a locally brewed drink with hints of honey and citrus, perfect for warming the bones after a long journey. After their meal, an older man entered the inn, his robes marking him as someone of importance, perhaps a scholar or a sage. His eyes were sharp, and there was a knowing look about him as he moved toward the bar.

Elion nudged Zephyros. "He might be the one."

Zephyros nodded in agreement. "Let's find out."

As the man took a seat at the bar, Zephyros and Elion approached him, their movements measured and respectful. Zephyros spoke first, his voice calm and polite.

"Good evening, sir. My friend and I are travelers seeking knowledge of the lands ahead. We've heard rumors of a place called the Shadowed Vale, but its location eludes us. Perhaps you could help?"

The man looked up at them, his eyes sharp and appraising. For a moment, he said nothing, simply studying them with a gaze that seemed to see straight through them.

Finally, he donned a wry, knowing smile. "The Shadowed Vale, you say? That's not a place one finds on a map. It's hidden, protected by magic and the will of those who dwell there. But I've heard whispers…and I might be able to point you in the right direction."

Elion exchanged a glance with Zephyros, hope flickering in his eyes. "Anything you can tell us would be greatly appreciated."

The man nodded, motioning for them to sit. "Very well. Let's talk."

As they settled in for the conversation, the shadows lengthened outside the inn, the night growing darker as the two men inched closer to their goal, the Shadowed Vale, and with it the promise of vengeance and redemption.

CHAPTER 7

The early-morning light filtered through the windows of The Wanderer's Rest, casting a soft, golden glow over the inn's common room. Zephyros and Elion had risen early, eager to follow up on the leads provided by the man they had spoken with the night before. The town was still quiet, only a few early risers moving about the streets, where the air was cool and crisp.

As they stepped outside, the town had a different feel—a place where secrets were traded as casually as goods in the marketplace. The man at the bar had mentioned a few individuals who might have more information about the Shadowed Vale, and Zephyros and Elion wasted no time in seeking them out.

Their first stop was at a small herbalist's shop on the edge of town, where a wizened old woman greeted them with a knowing smile. Her shop was filled with the scent of dried herbs and the faint hum of magical energy, the shelves lined with jars of ingredients and potions.

"You seek the Vale," she said, her voice wheezy. "A place few find and fewer return from. It's protected by old magic, but there are ways to see what others cannot."

Zephyros leaned forward, intrigued. "What kind of magic?"

The woman's eyes twinkled. "The kind that requires more than skill. You need purpose, a reason to be there. The Vale reveals itself to those who have a destiny to fulfill. But be warned—the path is treacherous, and those who enter often face trials they are not prepared for."

Elion glanced at Zephyros, both understanding the gravity of what she spoke of. "Thank you," Elion said, offering her a few coins. "This information is invaluable."

The old woman took the coins with a nod. "May the spirits guide you."

They left the shop with more questions than answers but a clearer sense of what they were up against. As they continued their search, they spoke with a blacksmith who had once traveled near the Vale, a bard who claimed to have heard tales of its hidden paths, and a merchant who had traded with mysterious figures from the Vale. Each provided pieces of a puzzle that was slowly coming together.

By midday, Zephyros and Elion found themselves back at the inn, discussing their next steps over a simple meal. A modest spread of food lay between them: a bowl of thick vegetable stew, filled with chunks of carrots, potatoes, and leeks, accompanied by a small plate of crusty bread. The stew, simple yet flavorful, carried the warmth of fresh herbs, while the bread, though plain, had a satisfying crunch. A wedge of sharp cheese and a cup of watered-down ale completed the humble fare, the kind of meal that filled the stomach but left no room for indulgence.

"We've learned a lot, but there's still much we don't know," Elion said, his brow furrowed in thought. "The Vale is protected by powerful magic, but it sounds like we have a chance if we approach it with the right intent."

Zephyros nodded, his eyes distant as he considered their options. "We should stay another night, listen in on the conversations at the pub. There might be more information we can gather."

Elion agreed, and they settled in to wait for the evening, when the inn would once again fill with patrons.

As night fell, the common room of The Wanderer's Rest came alive with the hum of conversation and the clatter of mugs. Zephyros and Elion sat in a corner, nursing their drinks and listening intently to the chatter around them. The atmosphere was lively, but there was an undercurrent of tension, as if the town's inhabitants were on edge.

It wasn't long before they overheard something that caught their attention.

"Did you hear about the attempted assassination at the castle?" a man at a nearby table whispered to his companion, his voice low and conspiratorial.

Elion's ears perked up, and he subtly shifted his position to hear better.

"Aye," the other man replied. "They say two assassins got in, real shadows they were. Nearly killed the prince, but he escaped—barely. Rumor has it they kidnapped him."

Zephyros and Elion exchanged a glance, their interest piqued.

"What did they look like?" another asked.

"Dark elves, from the sound of it," the first man said. "One was tall with hair as white as snow, and the other was built like a mountain, with eyes like green fire. Dangerous, both of them."

Zephyros's grip tightened around his mug. There was no mistaking it. The descriptions matched Kumori and Iwa.

The conversation continued, with the men speculating about the motives behind the attack. Some believed it was a political move, while others thought it was a personal vendetta. But the most interesting theory came from an older man sitting at the bar.

"Mark my words," he said, his voice carrying across the room. "This wasn't an assassination attempt. The queen's involved in this somehow. She's been acting strange lately, more secretive than usual. And that wizard she's always with… Something's not right there."

Elion frowned, remembering the description of the wizard they had seen with the queen. "They think the prince was kidnapped, but that's what the queen wants them to believe," he muttered to Zephyros.

Zephyros nodded, his mind racing. "Kumori and Iwa didn't kidnap the prince. They probably found out what was going on and decided to take him somewhere safe. We need to find them."

Elion agreed. "If they've taken the prince, they might be heading to the Vale. It's the only place they'd be able to hide him from whatever dark force is controlling the emperor."

They spent the rest of the evening gathering as much information as they could, listening to every scrap of gossip and rumor. The more they heard, the clearer their path became.

By the time the common room began to empty, Zephyros and Elion had made their decision. They would head toward the castle, hoping to intercept Kumori and Iwa, and perhaps even find a way to help the prince.

As they climbed the stairs to their room, the urgency of the coming journey settled over them. The Shadowed Vale was becoming the center of a much larger conflict, one that involved powerful forces they were only beginning to understand.

"Tomorrow, we head toward the castle," Zephyros said as they prepared for bed. "We need to move quickly if we're going to catch up to them."

Elion nodded, his thoughts already turning to the journey ahead. "And once we find them, we'll figure out how to stop whatever's happening in that palace."

They settled in for the night, their minds heavy with the knowledge that the path they were on was fraught with danger. But they were determined to see it through, no matter the cost. As the town slept, it was unaware of the storm that was brewing beyond its borders.

CHAPTER 8

The morning air was crisp and cool as Zephyros and Elion made their final preparations to leave the small town. The sun had begun to rise, casting long shadows across the cobblestone streets as the townsfolk slowly stirred to life. Zephyros was focused, his mind set on the journey ahead, while Elion methodically checked their supplies, ensuring they had everything they needed for the trek to the castle.

As they browsed through the market to gather the last of their provisions, a merchant—a man with a grizzled beard and sharp eyes—stepped forward from his stall and approached them. He held out a small, folded piece of parchment.

"A word of caution," the merchant said in a low voice, his eyes darting around as if to make sure no one was listening. "Take this. And be careful."

Zephyros took the note, his brow furrowing. "What's this about?"

The merchant gave a slight shake of his head. "Read it when you're away from prying eyes. Not everyone in this town is to be trusted."

The merchant turned and disappeared back into the crowd, leaving Zephyros and Elion to exchange a concerned glance.

Once they were out of sight of the market, Zephyros unfolded the note. The handwriting was hurried, but the message was clear. It read, "You are being watched. Be wary—some who enter this town have their own agendas. Trust no one."

Elion's eyes narrowed as he read over Zephyros's shoulder. "Seems we're attracting more attention than we thought."

Zephyros nodded, folding the note and tucking it away. "We need to be on our guard. Whatever we're getting into, it's bigger than just us."

With the note's warning fresh in their minds, they quickly finished gathering their supplies and prepared to leave the town. As they approached the outskirts, the road ahead stretched out before them, winding through the dense forests that lay between the town and the castle.

But as they were about to pass the last of the town's buildings, a group of rough-looking men stepped out from the shadows of an alley, blocking their path. They were a motley crew—scruffy, armed with crude weapons, and each wearing a wicked grin.

"Well, well," the leader of the group sneered, stepping forward with a swagger. "Look what we have here, boys. A couple of fancy travelers, ripe for the picking."

Elion's hand instinctively moved to the hilt of his sword, while Zephyros's eyes narrowed. "We're just passing through," Zephyros said calmly. "You'd be wise to step aside."

The leader laughed, a harsh, grating sound. "Oh, I don't think so. See, we've had a slow morning, and you two look like you're carrying more than enough to make it worth our while. Hand it over, and maybe we'll let you walk away."

Zephyros and Elion exchanged a glance. They didn't want a fight, but it seemed one was inevitable.

"We gave you a chance," Elion said, his voice steely. "Now, you'll regret not taking it."

Before the bandits could react, Zephyros moved with lightning speed, his hand snapping up as he summoned a gust of wind that sent the leader stumbling back. Elion drew his sword, the blade flashing in the morning light as he stepped forward to meet the nearest bandit.

The fight was quick but intense. Zephyros wielded his storm magic with precision, bolts of lightning arcing from his hands to strike down each bandit who dared to challenge him. The air crackled with energy as he moved, each strike a testament to his power. Elion, meanwhile, fought with the grace of a seasoned warrior, his sword dancing through the air as he parried blows and countered with deadly accuracy.

The bandits quickly realized they were outmatched, but it was too late. One by one, they fell, either knocked unconscious by Zephyros's magic or disarmed and defeated by Elion's blade.

As the last of the bandits crumpled to the ground, breathing heavily, Zephyros and Elion stood victorious. But before they could catch their breaths, a slow clap echoed through the clearing.

"Impressive," a voice drawled, smooth and dripping with disdain.

Both men turned to see a figure emerging from the shadows of the trees. The newcomer was tall and lean, dressed in dark, form-fitting clothes that allowed him to blend seamlessly with his surroundings. His face was partially obscured by a hood, but his eyes—glowing with a faint, unsettling purple light—were clearly visible.

The assassin took a step closer, a wicked-looking dagger in his hand. "The goddess Umbra sends her regards, Zephyros. She's not too pleased with your little quest for vengeance."

Zephyros's heart skipped a beat as he recognized the name. Umbra, the Goddess of the Night, one of the very deities he had sworn to defy.

"You've been sent to kill me," Zephyros said, his voice deceptively calm.

The assassin smirked. "That's the idea, but after watching you two in action, I have to say… It's not going to be easy. Still, orders are orders."

Suddenly, the assassin lunged, moving with a speed and agility that was almost inhuman. Zephyros and Elion sprang into action, the battle beginning in earnest now.

The assassin was a formidable opponent, his movements fluid and precise as he dodged Zephyros's lightning and parried Elion's strikes. But Zephyros and Elion fought with the strength of men who had something to lose—something worth protecting.

Zephyros unleashed the full fury of his storm magic, lightning striking the ground around the assassin, forcing him to constantly stay on the move. Elion pressed the attack with his sword, each swing aimed to corner the assassin and limit his options.

Despite his skill, the assassin was gradually overwhelmed. A particularly powerful bolt of lightning from Zephyros finally struck true, sending the assassin crashing to the ground, his dagger clattering away.

Breathing heavily, the assassin looked up at Zephyros, his smirk replaced with a grimace of pain. "You… You might have won this round, but the gods and goddesses are watching. They won't let you succeed. They'll do everything in their power to stop you."

Zephyros stepped closer, his eyes blazing with determination. "Let them try."

Before Zephyros could finish him off, the assassin's eyes flashed with defiance. "This isn't over," he hissed, and with a sudden burst of speed, he reached into his cloak and shattered a small, dark crystal against the ground. Instantly, a thick cloud of black smoke erupted, obscuring him from view.

When the smoke cleared, the assassin was gone, leaving only the faint echo of his final words hanging in the air.

Zephyros and Elion stood in silence for a moment, the weight of the assassin's warning pressing down on them.

Elion finally sheathed his sword, his expression grim. "If the gods and goddesses are truly watching us, then this has become more dangerous than we imagined."

Zephyros nodded, his resolve hardening. "We'll face whatever they throw at us. We have to."

With that, they continued on their journey, the road ahead now fraught with even more peril. But they were determined, and their goal remained unchanged: to reach the castle, find Kumori and Iwa, and put an end to the darkness that threatened their world.

As they walked, the sun climbed higher in the sky, casting their shadows on the path before them. The battle had been won, but the war was only beginning.

CHAPTER 9

The road from the small town where Zephyros and Elion had their encounter with the assassin led them through a landscape that was as varied as it was beautiful. The land of Elarion was rich with natural wonders, from rolling hills covered in wildflowers to dense forests where ancient trees reached up to the sky, their branches woven together in a canopy of green.

As they journeyed onward, the terrain began to change. The gentle hills gave way to more rugged land, where the earth was rocky and the paths more treacherous. The air grew cooler as they climbed higher, the distant peaks of the Stonefang Mountains rising up before them, their snow-capped summits glinting in the morning sun.

Zephyros walked with a purposeful stride, his eyes constantly scanning the horizon. Elion kept pace beside him. The encounter with the assassin had left them both on edge, and the note from the merchant still weighed heavily on their minds.

As they traveled, Elion delved into his thoughts for some time. "Zephyros," he began, his voice contemplative, "what do you think is really going on here? With the emperor, the queen, and now the gods themselves taking an interest in us?"

Zephyros's gaze remained forward, his expression stern. "I think we're dealing with forces far beyond anything we've encountered before. The gods and goddesses have always been distant, but now it seems they're directly interfering in the mortal realm. And that can only mean one thing. Whatever's happening in the capital, it's threatening their power."

Elion nodded slowly. "The emperor being controlled by some dark entity from the Abyss... It's almost too much to believe. And yet it makes a twisted kind of sense. If the gods are threatened, then we're dealing with something ancient, something powerful."

Zephyros glanced at Elion, his eyes narrowing. "And that's why we can't fail. Whatever this darkness is, it's spreading, and if we don't stop it, it could consume everything."

They walked in silence for a while longer, the gravity of their situation weighing heavily on both of them. The path they were on was narrow and winding, carved into the side of a rocky hill that overlooked a wide, glistening lake. The water was still and clear, reflecting the sky like a mirror.

As they approached the lake, they noticed a lone traveler standing at its edge, his face drawn with frustration. He was a middle-aged man, his clothes simple but sturdy, and he seemed to be searching the water intently.

Zephyros and Elion exchanged a glance before approaching the man. "Is something wrong?" Zephyros asked, his voice carrying easily across the quiet landscape.

The man looked up, relief flashing in his eyes as he saw them. "Oh, thank the gods! I could use some help. I dropped something valuable into the lake, and I've been trying to fish it out, but it's too deep for me to reach."

Elion stepped closer, peering into the water. "What did you drop?"

"A small chest," the man explained. "It's got some heirlooms in it, nothing of great value to anyone else, but they're important to me. It slipped out of my pack when I was resting here, and now it's sunk to the bottom."

Zephyros looked at the lake, his mind already calculating. The water was deep, but it was calm, and he could sense the currents beneath the surface. "I think I can help with that," he said, stepping forward.

The traveler watched with wide eyes as Zephyros raised his hand, his fingers spreading as he called upon the power of the storm. The air around them crackled with energy, and the surface of the lake began to ripple as Zephyros concentrated. Slowly, the water churned, and a faint glow appeared beneath the surface, growing brighter as Zephyros focused his magic.

With a sweeping motion, Zephyros drew the water upward, and the small chest emerged from the depths, carried by a column of swirling liquid. The traveler gasped in amazement as the chest was gently deposited on the shore, water cascading off it in rivulets.

"By the gods," the man breathed, dropping to his knees beside the chest. "Thank you so much! I don't know how I can ever repay you."

Zephyros waved off the man's gratitude, a small smile tugging at the corner of his lips. "No need for repayment. Be more careful next time."

The man nodded vigorously, still in awe of what he had witnessed. "I will. You're a true miracle worker, sir. I can't thank you enough."

As the man carefully packed the chest back into his belongings, Zephyros and Elion glanced at each other, silently communicating that there was no need to rush off.

"Have you traveled this way recently?" Elion asked casually. "We're looking for some acquaintances who might have passed by."

The traveler nodded as he secured his pack. "Aye, I've been on the road for a few days now. You know, I did see a couple of fellows who might be who you're looking for. Dark elves, both of them. One tall with white hair, the other built like a bear."

Zephyros and Elion exchanged a knowing glance. "That sounds like them," Zephyros said. "Do you know where they were headed?"

The traveler pointed down the road. "They were heading in the same direction you are, toward Stonehaven. That's the big dwarven city past the mountains. If you keep moving, you might catch up to them."

"Thank you," Elion said, genuinely grateful. "You've been a big help."

The traveler waved them off, already preparing to continue his journey. "Safe travels to you both. And thank you again for your help."

As the traveler disappeared down the road in the opposite direction, Zephyros and Elion resumed their journey, their spirits lifted by the knowledge that they were on the right path.

* * *

Meanwhile, Kumori, Iwa, and Aethas were also heading toward Stonehaven. The path they took was more direct, cutting through dense forests and across fast-moving streams that crisscrossed the land. The forest was alive with the sounds of birds and rustling leaves, the air fresh with the scent of pine and earth.

Kumori moved with purpose, his senses attuned to every sound and movement in the forest. Iwa followed close behind, his massive frame seemingly unaffected by the rough terrain. Despite their careful pace, both men were alert, knowing that danger could be lurking around any corner.

Aethas struggled to keep pace with the two assassins, who moved so gracefully they seemed part of the landscape itself. Kumori kept him at a distance—close enough to monitor Aethas, yet far enough that he couldn't overhear the conversation he was having with Iwa.

"This place is beautiful," Iwa remarked as they navigated a narrow path that wound through a grove of ancient trees. "It's easy to forget what we're running from."

Kumori nodded, his expression thoughtful. "The beauty of this land makes you realize what's at stake. If we fail, all of this could be consumed by darkness."

Iwa glanced at his friend, concern etched on his face. "Do you think the prince can really help us? That Varun will know what to do?"

Kumori sighed, his eyes distant. "I don't know, Iwa. Aethas is strong but also young, untested. Varun is wise, but even he hasn't faced something like this. The Abyss is ancient, and its power is beyond anything we've seen."

They walked in silence for a while, lost in their own thoughts. The forest gradually thinned out as they climbed higher into the mountains, the path becoming steeper and more treacherous. The air grew colder, and the ground beneath their feet became rocky and uneven.

Eventually, the forest gave way entirely to a vast, rocky landscape dotted with hardy shrubs and the occasional tree clinging to the mountainside. In the distance, they could see the towering peaks of the Stonefang Mountains, their jagged summits piercing the sky.

"We're getting close," Kumori said, his eyes narrowing as he scanned the horizon. "Stonehaven is just beyond those peaks."

Iwa nodded, his gaze shifting to the mountains ahead. "Good. I'm ready to rest in a real bed for once."

Kumori chuckled, a rare sound that lightened the mood. "You and me both, my friend."

As they continued their journey, the path led them through a narrow mountain pass, the walls of stone towering high above them. The wind howled through the pass, carrying with it the scent of snow and the promise of colder weather ahead.

Eventually, they emerged from the pass to find themselves overlooking a vast valley. Below them, nestled into the side of the mountain was the dwarven city of Stonehaven. The city was a marvel of engineering, carved directly into the rock of the mountain, with massive stone towers and battlements rising up to meet the sky.

The entrance to Stonehaven was a massive gate set into the mountain's face, guarded by imposing dwarven sentinels. The gate was flanked by two enormous statues of ancient dwarven kings, their expressions stern as they gazed out over the valley.

Kumori and Iwa made their way down the winding path that led to the city's entrance, their steps echoing off the stone walls. As they approached the gate, they were met by a pair of dwarven guards, their armor gleaming in the fading light.

"Halt!" one of the guards barked, his voice gruff. "State your business in Stonehaven."

Kumori stepped forward, his posture calm and respectful. "We're travelers seeking shelter for the night. We mean no harm."

The guards exchanged a glance before nodding. "Very well. Welcome to Stonehaven. But mind your manners. We don't tolerate troublemakers."

The massive gates creaked open, revealing the bustling city beyond.

Stonehaven was a sight to behold. The city was vast, with streets that wound through the mountain, lined with stone buildings that were both sturdy and beautifully crafted. The architecture was distinctly dwarven, with angular designs and intricate carvings that adorned every surface. The city was alive with activity, dwarves going about their business, merchants hawking their wares, and the sounds of hammers ringing out from the many forges scattered throughout the city.

The three of them made their way through the crowded streets, marveling at the sheer scale of the city. Stone bridges spanned deep chasms, connecting different parts of the city, and massive stone pillars supported the towering ceilings high above. The air was filled with the scent of metal and stone, a reminder of the dwarves' industrious nature.

As they walked, they passed by numerous taverns and inns, each one bustling with patrons. The dwarves of Stonehaven were known for their hospitality, and it was clear that the city was a hub for travelers from all across the land.

"We should find a place to rest," Iwa suggested, his eyes scanning the many taverns. "We'll need our strength for whatever comes next."

Kumori nodded in agreement, his thoughts already turning to their next move. "Let's find somewhere discreet. We don't want to draw too much attention."

They eventually settled on a modest-looking tavern called The Iron Flask, its sign swinging gently in the evening breeze. The tavern was less crowded than some of the others, and it had the look of a place where one could blend in easily.

As they entered, the warmth of the hearth greeted them, along with the smell of roasting meat and freshly baked bread. The interior was cozy, with wooden beams overhead and stone walls that gave the place a solid, welcoming feel. The patrons were a mix of dwarves and other travelers, all enjoying their meals and drinks in relative peace.

They found a table near the back, away from prying eyes, and settled in. They ordered a hearty dwarven meal of spiced boar sausages, dark rye bread slathered with butter, and a side of pickled vegetables, paired with a round of strong, frothy ale, eager to relax after their long journey. As they ate, they spoke in low voices, discussing their plans and what they had learned in the capital. The atmosphere in the tavern was comfortable, but both men remained alert, knowing that they couldn't afford to let their guard down.

Meanwhile, as the sun dipped below the horizon, Zephyros and Elion finally reached Stonehaven. The journey through the mountains had been long and arduous, but the sight of the dwarven city brought a sense of relief. They had been traveling for days, and the promise of shelter was a welcome one.

The massive gates of Stonehaven loomed before them, and after a brief exchange with the guards, they were allowed entry. The city was as impressive as they had imagined, its grandeur a testament to the skill and craftsmanship of the dwarves.

As they passed through the city, the sounds and sights of Stonehaven filled their senses. The streets were crowded with people of all races, the dwarves mingling with humans, elves, and other travelers. The city had a lively, bustling energy, with the clatter of hooves on stone and the hum of conversation creating a symphony of activity.

Elion looked around in awe, taking in the scale of the city. "This place is incredible. I've never seen anything like it."

Zephyros nodded, his eyes scanning the crowd. "The dwarves have always been master builders. But we're not here to admire the architecture. We need to find Kumori and Iwa."

As they walked, Zephyros noticed a familiar figure entering a tavern up ahead. He squinted, his eyes narrowing as he recognized Kumori's distinctive white hair and Iwa's imposing frame.

"There," Zephyros said, pointing toward the tavern. "They just went inside."

Elion followed his gaze, his expression sharpening. "Let's go. We need to talk to them."

They headed toward The Iron Flask, their minds focused on the encounter that was about to take place. They didn't know what to expect, but they knew that whatever happened next would be crucial to their mission.

As they reached the door of the tavern, they exchanged a glance, each man silently steeling himself for what was to come. Then, without another word, they stepped inside, the warmth and noise of the tavern enveloping them as they prepared to confront the two dark elves who had unknowingly become their allies in the battle against the darkness.

There, they stood at the entrance of The Iron Flask, their eyes locked on the table where Kumori, Iwa, and Aethas sat, unaware of the figures watching them from across the room.

CHAPTER 10

Kumori and Iwa were deep in conversation, their expressions serious as they discussed their next steps. The tavern was bustling with activity, voices blending into a low hum that filled the air.

Zephyros exchanged a glance with Elion, a silent understanding passing between them. This was the moment they had been waiting for, the moment when their paths would finally cross with those of the two assassins they had been following.

They approached the table, moving with the quiet confidence of men who had faced countless dangers and emerged victorious. As they neared, Kumori's sharp eyes flicked up, immediately locking onto the two newcomers. Iwa noticed the shift in his companion's demeanor and turned to see what had caught his attention.

For a moment, the four men simply stared at each other.

Zephyros spoke, "Kumori, I presume. And you must be Iwa. We need to talk."

Kumori's eyes narrowed slightly, but he didn't reach for his weapons. "And who are you?"

"I'm Zephyros," he replied. "This is Elion. We've been looking for you."

Iwa's hand moved subtly closer to his dagger, but Kumori held up a hand to stop him. "Looking for us? Why?"

Elion took a step forward, his posture relaxed but ready. "We're on the same side, or at least we could be. We know about the situation at the capital—the emperor, the queen, and the creature from the Abyss."

At the mention of the Abyss, Kumori's expression darkened. "So you know what's going on. That still doesn't explain why you've been following us."

Zephyros pulled out a chair and sat down, motioning for Elion to do the same. "We have our own mission, and it led us to you. We believe that whatever is happening in the capital is connected to something much larger—something that threatens not just the empire but the entire world."

Kumori and Iwa exchanged a glance, a silent conversation passing between them. Finally, Kumori said, "We're listening."

For the next hour, the two groups shared their stories. Zephyros and Elion recounted their journey, the assassination attempt on Zephyros, and the warnings they had received about the gods and goddesses watching them. Kumori and Iwa in turn explained their mission to protect Prince Aethas and their decision to take him to the Shadowed Vale for help.

As the conversation continued, the tension in the air slowly began to dissipate. While there was still an underlying wariness between the two groups, they began to realize that their goals were more aligned than they had initially thought.

"So," Kumori said, leaning back in his chair, "you're saying that the gods themselves are trying to stop you? And that this creature from the Abyss is part of a larger plan?"

Zephyros nodded. "That's what it seems like. The gods are afraid of something, and they're willing to go to great lengths to stop us from finding out what it is."

Elion leaned forward, his eyes fixed on Kumori. "We need to get to the Shadowed Vale. Whatever's happening, Varun might be the only one who can help us understand it—and stop it."

Kumori was silent for a moment, pondering. "The Vale is protected for a reason. Outsiders aren't usually welcomed, and Varun doesn't trust easily. Bringing you there could cause more harm than good."

Zephyros's expression was unreadable, but his eyes were hard. "We don't have a choice. If we don't work together, everything we're fighting for could be lost."

Iwa, who had been listening intently, finally spoke up, "He's right, Kumori. We can't do this alone. If they're willing to help, we should at least consider it."

Kumori looked at Iwa then at Prince Aethas, who had been quietly absorbing everything that was being said. The young prince's eyes were filled with a determination that belied his youth.

"I'll do whatever it takes to save my father and stop this darkness," Aethas said. "If that means trusting them, then so be it."

The table fell into a contemplative silence as each man considered the implications of their next move. Despite their shared goals, there was still an unspoken tension between them—an uncertainty about whether they could truly trust one another.

Finally, Zephyros stood up. "We should all get some rest. Tomorrow, we'll decide our next steps."

Kumori nodded, though his expression remained guarded. "Agreed. We'll think it over."

The two groups parted ways, each retreating to their respective rooms in the tavern. But in bed that night, Zephyros's mind was far from restful. He knew that Kumori and Iwa were right to be cautious, but he also knew that they couldn't afford to waste time. The forces aligned against them were powerful, and they needed every advantage they could get.

That was why Zephyros quietly cast a spell—one that would allow him to track Kumori and Iwa's movements. It was a subtle spell, one that wouldn't be easily detected, but it would give him the information he needed if they chose to go their separate ways in the morning.

Elion, lying in the bed across the room, spoke softly in the darkness. "Are you sure about this, Zephyros? We're taking a big risk."

Zephyros grumbled, "We don't have a choice, Elion. We need to know what they're planning. We can't let them go off on their own, not when so much is at stake."

Elion sighed but didn't argue. "I hope you're right."

They both fell into a fitful sleep, their minds racing with thoughts of the days to come.

The morning dawned with a soft, pale light filtering through the small windows of the tavern. The town of Stonehaven was already alive with activity, the sounds of hammers on anvils and the murmur of voices filling the air.

Zephyros and Elion were up early, gathering their supplies and preparing for the next leg of their journey. The tension from the night before still lingered, but they moved with purpose, knowing that they couldn't afford to lose any time.

As they traversed the bustling streets of Stonehaven, they passed by the many shops and stalls that lined the city's main thoroughfare. The dwarven craftsmanship was evident in everything from the weapons and armor on display to the finely woven fabrics and intricately carved stonework.

Elion, who had a deep appreciation for fine craftsmanship, couldn't help but admire the skill that had gone into creating the items on display. "The dwarves really are master artisans," he remarked, running a hand over the polished surface of a stone carving.

Zephyros nodded, though his mind was elsewhere. "They are. But we need to stay focused. We have to be ready to move quickly if Kumori and Iwa decide to leave without us."

As they continued through the market, Zephyros kept a subtle watch on the spell he had cast the night before. It was a simple tracking spell, designed to alert him if Kumori and Iwa left the town. So far, there had been no indication that they were on the move, but Zephyros remained vigilant.

After gathering the supplies they needed—food, water, and a few additional items for the journey ahead—they returned to the tavern to find that Kumori, Iwa, and Prince Aethas were also preparing to leave.

Kumori looked up as they approached, his expression unreadable. "We're heading out," he said simply.

Zephyros nodded. "We'll be leaving soon as well."

There was a brief, awkward silence as the two groups regarded each other. Despite their shared experiences from the night before, there was still an undercurrent of tension.

Finally, Kumori turned and led his group out of the tavern, with Iwa and Aethas following close behind. Zephyros watched them go, his mind racing with thoughts of what they should do next.

"They're leaving," Elion said quietly. "Should we follow them?"

Zephyros nodded, his decision already made. "We'll give them a little time, then we'll follow. I need to know where they're going."

They finished their preparations and waited for the right moment to set out. It wasn't long before they left the tavern, their footsteps echoing on the stone streets as they made their way out of Stonehaven.

The road ahead was rugged and wild, leading them deeper into the heart of the mountains. The landscape around them was a stark contrast to the bustling city they had left behind. The towering peaks of the Stonefang Mountains loomed overhead, their craggy faces etched with deep crevices and jagged cliffs.

As they descended from the mountains, the land began to change once again. The rugged terrain gave way to dense forests, where the trees grew tall and close together, their branches forming a thick canopy that blocked out much of the sunlight. The forest was dark and shadowed, the air thick with the scent of damp earth and moss.

But there was something else about the forest, something that felt different from any other place they had been. The light that filtered through the trees had a peculiar quality to it, casting everything in a muted, almost ethereal glow. It wasn't inherently sinister, but there was a sense of shade, as if the forest was holding its breath, waiting for something to happen.

"This place feels…different," Elion remarked, his eyes scanning the shadows between the trees. "Not evil, but like it's watching us."

Zephyros nodded in agreement. "It's the magic of the Vale. We're getting close."

They continued through the forest, their senses heightened as they navigated the winding paths and overgrown trails. The silence of the forest was occasionally broken by the distant call of a bird or the rustle of leaves in the wind, but for the most part the world around them seemed wrapped in anticipation.

As they walked, Zephyros kept a close eye on the spell he had cast. It guided him like a compass, pointing him in the direction of Kumori and Iwa. They were getting closer with each passing hour, and Zephyros knew it was only a matter of time before they reached the entrance to the Shadowed Vale.

The journey through the forest was long and tiring, but Zephyros and Elion pressed on, determined to reach their destination. The landscape around them continued to shift and change, the trees growing thicker and the light dimmer as they delved deeper into the heart of the forest.

Finally, after what felt like hours of walking, they saw it—a break in the trees that revealed a narrow, rocky path leading up to a steep hillside. The path was lined with ancient stones, worn smooth by time, and at the top they could just make out the entrance to a hidden valley, shrouded in mist and shadow.

"This must be it," Elion said, his voice filled with a mix of awe and apprehension. "The entrance to the Shadowed Vale."

Zephyros nodded, his eyes fixed on the path ahead. "We need to be careful. The Vale is protected by powerful magic, and we don't know what we'll find inside."

As they began to ascend the path, Zephyros felt a subtle shift in the air around them, as if they were crossing an invisible threshold. The light grew even dimmer, and the shadows seemed to lengthen, stretching out like dark fingers reaching for them.

But they continued onward, their determination unwavering. They had come too far to turn back now.

At the top of the path, they paused, taking in the sight before them. The Shadowed Vale was a place of otherworldly beauty, where the natural world and magic intertwined in ways that defied understanding. The valley was filled with ancient trees, their branches twisted and gnarled, and the air was thick with the scent of wildflowers and earth.

But there was also a sense of danger, a feeling that they were being watched by unseen eyes. The shadows in the Vale were deep and ever-present, and the light that filtered through the mist was strange and haunting.

As they stood at the entrance to the Vale, Zephyros felt the spell he had cast shift slightly, guiding him toward a distant part of the valley. Kumori and Iwa were close.

"They're here," Zephyros said quietly. "We're on the right path."

Elion nodded, his eyes scanning the valley below. "Let's find them—and find out what happens next."

They began their descent into the Shadowed Vale, the shadows closing in around them as they moved deeper into the heart of the mystery that had brought them all together.

CHAPTER 11

The light of the morning sun struggled to pierce the thick canopy of the ancient forest as Kumori led the way through the dense undergrowth. The air was heavy with the scent of moss and damp earth, and the sounds of the forest—birds calling, leaves rustling—were muted.

The path they followed was narrow and winding, a faint trail that seemed to shift and change with every step, as if the forest itself was guiding them deeper into its embrace.

Kumori moved with the fluid grace of a shadow, his senses attuned to the subtle shifts in the environment around him. Behind him, Iwa followed closely, his massive frame surprisingly quiet as he navigated the rough terrain. Prince Aethas brought up the rear, his eyes wide as he took in the strange and mysterious world around him.

The forest they had entered was unlike any Aethas had ever seen. The trees were ancient, their trunks thick and gnarled, their branches twisted into strange, almost otherworldly shapes. The light that filtered through the canopy was dim and diffuse, casting everything in a pale, almost ghostly glow. It wasn't dark, but there was a sense of shade—a feeling that the forest was alive with secrets, watching them with unseen eyes.

"This place… It feels different," Aethas remarked, his voice barely above a whisper. "There's something about it."

Kumori glanced back at the prince, his expression unreadable. "The forest is old. It's seen things, lived through things, that we can't even begin to understand. It's not hostile, but it's not welcoming either. It's a place where shadows linger."

Iwa nodded in agreement. "It's the magic of the Vale. We're getting close. The forest knows it, and it's reacting to us."

Aethas fell silent, his thoughts turning inward as he considered what was ahead. The Shadowed Vale was a place of legend, a hidden refuge for those who sought to escape the eyes of the world. But it was also a place of danger, protected by powerful magic and inhabited by those who did not welcome outsiders.

As they continued deeper into the forest, the path grew steeper, winding its way up the side of a hill. The trees here were even older, their trunks twisted and bent, as if they had been shaped by some ancient force. The undergrowth was thick, the ground covered in a carpet of ferns and moss that muffled their footsteps.

Kumori's mind was focused, his thoughts sharp as he considered the path ahead. The Shadowed Vale was close—he could feel it in the air, in the way the forest seemed to press in around them. But there was also a sense of unease, a feeling that something was watching them from the shadows.

He paused at the top of the hill, his eyes scanning the landscape below. The valley stretched out before them, shrouded in mist and shadow. It was a place of haunting beauty, where the natural world and magic intertwined in ways that defied understanding. The air was thick with the scent of wildflowers and earth, and the light that filtered through the mist was strange and haunting.

"We're close," Kumori said quietly. "The entrance to the Vale is ahead."

Iwa moved up beside him, his eyes narrowed as he surveyed the valley. "Do you think they'll let us in?"

Kumori's expression was grim. "Varun knows we're coming. He'll let us in, but he won't be happy about it."

Aethas looked between the two dark elves, a hint of apprehension in his eyes. "And what about them?" he asked, his voice tense. "Zephyros and Elion—they're probably following us."

Kumori sighed, his gaze turning back to the valley below. "They're determined. They'll find a way to track us, even if we try to lose them. But we can't worry about that now. Our priority is getting you to Varun and figuring out what to do next."

Aethas nodded, though the tension in his shoulders didn't ease. He knew that they were walking into a situation fraught with danger and uncertainty, but there was no turning back now. The fate of his father—and perhaps the entire empire—rested on their shoulders.

The descent into the valley was slow and cautious. The path was narrow and treacherous, winding through dense thickets and over rocky outcrops. The mist that hung over the valley was thick and clinging, making it difficult to see more than a few feet ahead.

As they moved deeper into the valley, the sense of being watched grew stronger. The shadows seemed to shift and move at the edges of their vision.

Kumori remained focused, his senses attuned to every sound and movement. He knew that the Vale was protected by powerful magic that could twist and change reality itself. But he also knew that they had no choice but to press on. The answers they sought were within the Vale.

Finally, after what felt like hours of walking, they reached the entrance to the Shadowed Vale. The path ended at a steep cliff face, where a narrow crevice in the rock led into the darkness beyond. The entrance was hidden, almost invisible to those who didn't know where to look, but Kumori recognized it immediately.

"This is it," he muttered. "The entrance to the Vale." Iwa stepped forward, his expression serious. "Are you ready, Prince?"

Aethas nodded, though his eyes were wide with both fear and determination. "Let's do this."

They stepped into the crevice, the darkness swallowing them as they entered.

The inside of the Vale was unlike anything they had ever seen. The valley was vast and filled with towering trees that seemed to stretch endlessly into the sky. The light was dim and otherworldly. The air was thick with the scent of damp earth and the sound of distant waterfalls. But there was also a sense of danger, a feeling that the very land itself was alive, watching them with unseen eyes. The shadows in the Vale were deep and ever-present, and the path ahead was shrouded in mist and uncertainty.

As they made their way deeper in, Kumori couldn't shake the feeling that they were being followed. He paused for a moment, listening intently, but the only sounds were the rustle of leaves and the distant call of a bird.

"Something's not right," he said quietly, his eyes scanning the shadows. "We're not alone."

Iwa's hand went to his weapon, his eyes narrowing. "What do you mean?"

Kumori shook his head, his expression tense. "I don't know, but we need to be careful. The Vale is full of secrets, and not all of them are friendly."

They continued onward, their senses on high alert. The path wound deeper into the valley, leading them through dense thickets and over narrow bridges that spanned deep chasms. As they neared the center of the Vale, the path opened up into a wide clearing. In the center of the clearing stood a massive, ancient tree, its roots twisting and coiling like the tendrils of some giant beast. The tree was surrounded by a ring of stones, each one etched with strange, glowing runes.

"This is the heart of the Vale," Kumori said. "This is where Varun will meet us."

Aethas looked around in awe, his eyes wide as he took in the sight before him. "This place… It's incredible."

Kumori nodded, though his expression remained serious. "It's also dangerous. The magic here is strong and hostile to outsiders." They approached the tree, their steps cautious and deliberate. The air around them seemed to hum with energy, and the shadows seemed to shift and move, as if alive with some unseen force.

As they reached the center of the clearing, Kumori felt a powerful, ancient presence that seemed to radiate from the very ground beneath their feet. He knew that Varun was near, that the guardian of the Vale was watching them even now.

"Varun," Kumori called out, "we've come as you requested."

For a moment, there was only silence. Then, from the shadows of the tree, a figure emerged—a tall, imposing figure draped in dark robes, his eyes glowing with an eerie, otherworldly light. Varun, the guardian of the Shadowed Vale, stepped forward, his gaze fixed on Kumori and his companions. His presence was overwhelming, a force of nature that seemed to command the very air around him.

"You have come," Varun said, his voice deep and resonant. "But you have also brought outsiders into the Vale. Explain yourselves."

Kumori stepped forward. "We had no choice, Varun. Prince Aethas needs our help. His father, the emperor, is under the control of a dark force from the Abyss. We believe that force is connected to the gods themselves, and we need your guidance to stop it."

Varun's gaze shifted to Aethas, his eyes narrowing as he studied the young prince. "You bring grave news, Kumori. The Vale is a place of refuge, but it is also a place of great responsibility. To bring outsiders here is to risk exposing the secrets we have guarded for centuries."

Kumori held Varun's gaze, unwavering. "I understand the risk, but this situation is beyond anything we've faced before. If this darkness spreads, it won't just be the empire that falls—it will be the entire world. We need your help, and we need it now."

Varun's eyes flickered with something unreadable, and for a moment he was silent, as if weighing Kumori's words against the centuries of tradition and caution that had protected the Shadowed Vale.

He turned his gaze to Aethas, his expression inscrutable. "And you, young prince, do you understand the gravity of the situation you have brought to our doorstep? The Vale is not a place for those who seek power or glory. It is a sanctuary, a place where the balance of the world is maintained. Why should we risk that balance for you?"

Aethas swallowed but didn't waver. He stepped forward, meeting Varun's gaze, I don't seek power or glory. I seek to save my father and to stop the darkness that threatens us all. I know the risk I'm asking you to take, but I have no other choice. If you help me, I will do whatever it takes to protect the Vale and repay the debt I owe you."

Varun studied Aethas for a long moment, his gaze piercing, as if he were looking into the very soul of the young prince. Then, slowly, he nodded. "Very well," Varun said, his voice deep and resonant. "I will offer you my guidance. But know this—once you enter the Vale, there is no turning back. The path you walk is fraught with danger, and the choices you make here will determine the fate of more than just your father."

Aethas nodded, his resolve unshaken. "I understand."

Turning back to Kumori and Iwa, Varun's expression softening slightly. "You have done well to bring him here, but your task is not yet complete. There are trials ahead that will test your strength, your resolve, and your loyalty. Be prepared." Kumori and Iwa both nodded gravely. They knew that the path ahead would be difficult, but they were ready to face whatever challenges awaited them.

Varun stepped back, seeming to blend into the shadows of the great tree behind him. "Rest now, for the journey ahead is long and perilous. Tomorrow, we will begin the trials, and the true nature of the darkness you face will be revealed." He disappeared into the shadows, leaving Kumori, Iwa, and Aethas standing in the clearing, the weight of his words hanging heavy in the air.

Kumori turned to Aethas. "You heard him. This isn't going to be easy, and there's no guarantee we'll all make it out of this alive."

Aethas nodded, his face set in determination. "I know, but I have to try. For my father, for the empire, and for all of us."

Iwa placed a hand on Aethas's shoulder, offering a rare smile. "We'll stand by you, Prince. We've come this far together, and we'll see it through to the end."

As they began to set up camp for the night, the sense of being watched remained, but it was no longer a malevolent presence. It was as if the Vale itself was acknowledging their resolve, testing their worthiness to walk the path that was ahead.

* * *

Zephyros and Elion had finally reached the entrance to the Shadowed Vale, the dark forest seemed to loom over them as they stood before the narrow crevice that led into the hidden valley. The spell that Zephyros had cast to track Kumori and Iwa was still active, guiding them to this exact spot.

"This must be it, the entrance to the Vale," Elion said, his voice hushed as he took in the sight before them. Zephyros nodded, his gaze fixed on the dark opening in the rock.

"We've come this far, and we can't turn back now. Whatever happens inside, we have to find a way to stop this darkness."

They entered the crevice, the shadows swallowing them as they made their way into the Vale. The darkness was almost palpable, pressing in around them as they navigated the narrow passage. But Zephyros's resolve was unshakable, and he led the way with confidence.

As they emerged into the Vale itself, they were met with a landscape that was both beautiful and eerie. The valley was filled with ancient trees, their branches twisted and gnarled, and the air was thick with the scent of wildflowers and earth. The light that filtered through the mist was strange and haunting, casting everything in a pale, ethereal glow.

Elion took in the sight with a mixture of awe and apprehension. "This place feels alive, like it's watching us."

Zephyros nodded, his gaze scanning the landscape. "The Vale is protected by powerful magic. We're walking through a living, breathing entity. We have to be careful."

They continued deeper into the Vale, following the trail left by Kumori and his companions. The path was winding and treacherous, leading them through dense thickets and over narrow bridges that spanned deep chasms. The shadows in the Vale were deep and ever-present, and the sense of being watched was stronger than ever.

Finally, after what felt like hours of walking, they reached the same clearing where Kumori and the others had met with Varun. The massive, ancient tree in the center of the clearing was a sight to behold, its roots twisting and coiling like the tendrils of some giant beast. The air around it seemed to hum with energy, and the shadows seemed to shift and move, as if alive with some unseen force. Zephyros approached the tree cautiously, his senses on high alert.

"This is where they stopped," he said quietly. "We're close."

Elion nodded, his eyes scanning the clearing. "Do you think they know we're here?"

Zephyros's expression was grim. "If they don't, they will soon. We need to be prepared for anything."

As they stood in the clearing, the shadows seemed to close in around them, the air growing colder and heavier. The Vale was testing them, and they knew that they would have to prove themselves worthy of the path they had chosen. But despite the tension, there was also a sense of purpose—a feeling that they were on the right path, that they were meant to be here.

CHAPTER 12

The grand hall of the imperial palace was filled with the somber toll of bells, their mournful sound echoing through the vast, marble-clad space. The once-vibrant tapestries that adorned the walls seemed muted, as if the very fabric of the palace had absorbed the gravity of the news that was about to be delivered. The courtiers and nobles, dressed in their finest black attire, gathered in hushed groups, their faces pale and drawn. Whispers filled the air, each one a tendril of speculation and fear that coiled through the crowd like a snake.

At the far end of the hall, upon a dais draped in the imperial colors of crimson and gold, stood Queen Selenia, the picture of regal composure, her dark hair perfectly coiffed, her expression a mask of sorrow that betrayed nothing of the truth. She wore a gown of deep, mourning black, its fabric shimmering faintly in the dim light of the hall. A heavy veil of lace obscured her face, adding to the air of tragedy that clung to her like a shroud.

The courtiers fell silent as the queen raised a hand, her slender fingers adorned with rings that glittered like tiny stars. She waited a moment, letting the stillness settle over the room, before she began to speak.

"My loyal subjects," Queen Selenia's voice rang out, clear and unwavering, though heavy with the perfect amount of grief, "it is with the heaviest of hearts that I stand before you today, to deliver news that no mother should ever have to speak."

The silence in the hall deepened, the air thick with anticipation. Every eye was on the queen, every ear straining to catch her next words.

"My beloved son, Prince Aethas, has been taken from us," she continued, her voice faltering enough to convey the depth of her sorrow. "He was cruelly murdered by assassins, vile creatures who have no regard for life, who would strike down an innocent for their own gain."

A collective gasp swept through the crowd, followed by a murmur of disbelief and outrage. The queen allowed the reaction to build, her own expression one of barely contained anguish.

"These assassins—these despicable creatures—took from us not just a prince but a young man with a bright future, a future that would have brought prosperity and peace to our empire. My heart is shattered, as is the heart of every mother, every father, every citizen of this great land."

Her words were carefully chosen, each one designed to stoke the flames of anger and sorrow among the assembled nobility. She needed their support, their blind loyalty, to further her own agenda.

But beneath the veil of sorrow and loss, Queen Selenia's mind was as sharp and calculating as ever. She knew that the announcement of Aethas's death would solidify her control over the empire. With the prince out of the way, there would be no obstacles to her true goal: seizing complete and unchallenged power.

She allowed her tears to fall then, crystalline droplets that glistened on her cheeks as she continued. "But we must not let this tragedy break us. We must stand together, stronger than ever, and bring these assassins to justice. They will pay for their crimes, and the memory of my son will be avenged."

The crowd erupted into applause and cries of support, the sound filling the grand hall as the courtiers pledged their loyalty to the queen and her cause. Selenia stood there, her tears glistening like diamonds, the perfect image of a grieving mother and a determined ruler.

As the noise in the hall grew louder, the queen turned slightly, her gaze flicking to the shadows at the edge of the dais. There, hidden from the view of the assembled nobility, stood the shadowed figure of the dark wizard who had become her closest advisor, the man with glowing purple eyes who had whispered to her of power beyond imagining.

Their eyes met, and a slight, almost imperceptible smile curled the corners of Selenia's lips. The wizard inclined his head in acknowledgment, his expression unreadable beneath the hood of his cloak. The ruse was working perfectly. Aethas's supposed death would pave the way for the queen to manipulate the empire as she saw fit. With the emperor under her control and the prince out of the picture, there was no one left to challenge her authority.

But there was more to her plan than seizing power. Selenia's alliance with the creature from the

Abyss was about more than control—it was about as-cending to something greater, something that would make her more than a queen. The dark forces she had aligned herself with promised her power beyond her wildest dreams, power that would elevate her to god-hood if she played her cards right.

As the courtiers continued to applaud and offer their sympathies, Queen Selenia allowed herself to bask in their adoration. They believed her, every one of them, and that was exactly what she needed. They would rally to her cause, follow her lead, and in doing so they would unknowingly play their part in the greater game she was orchestrating.

When the time was right, she would reveal her true intentions. But for now, she would continue to play the role of the grieving mother, the heartbroken queen, until the pieces of her plan were all in place. As the applause finally began to die down, Selenia stepped forward, raising her hands for silence. "I know that this news has shaken us all to our core," she said, her voice gentle now, almost maternal. "But I ask you to remain strong. We will honor Aethas's memory by ensuring that the empire he loved so dearly remains united, steadfast in the face of this terrible loss."

She paused, letting her words sink in. "I will not rest until the assassins who took my son from me are brought to justice. I will see them punished, and I will see our empire restored to its rightful glory." The crowd erupted into cheers, the sound became deafening in the grand hall. Selenia smiled, a small, sorrowful smile that perfectly conveyed her grief—and masked the satisfaction that bubbled beneath the surface.

As she turned to leave the dais, her veil swishing softly with the movement, she caught the eye of the dark wizard once more. He stepped forward, falling into place beside her as they made their way through the hidden passage at the back of the dais, away from the prying eyes of the court.

Once they were alone in the dimly lit corridor, the queen's demeanor shifted. The sorrowful mask she had worn in the grand hall fell away, replaced by a cold, calculating expression.

"It went exactly as planned," she said. "The court believes every word. They will follow me without question."

The dark wizard broached a cruel, knowing smile that would send a shiver down the spine of even the most hardened of men. "Of course they do. You are their queen, after all, and you play the role beautifully."

Selenia allowed herself a moment of satisfaction before her thoughts turned to the next steps in her plan. "Now we must ensure that Aethas is never found. The people must believe that he is truly gone."

The wizard nodded, his eyes glowing faintly in the darkness. "He is being hunted as we speak. My shadows will find him—and when they do, he will be dealt with."

The queen's smile widened, her eyes gleaming with anticipation. "Good. Everything is falling into place. Soon, the empire will be mine, and with it, the power I have been promised."

The wizard inclined his head in agreement. "And when the time comes, you will have more power than any mortal has ever known."

Selenia's smile was full of ambition, her eyes alight with the fire of her desires. "Let the gods and goddesses watch. They will see the rise of a new power, one that will reshape this world in my image."

They continued down the corridor, their footsteps echoing through the palace as they left behind the grand hall and the assembled nobility, who remained oblivious to the dark forces at play in their midst.

As they disappeared into the shadows, the bells of the palace continued to toll, their mournful sound a fitting accompaniment to the lies and deception that had been woven. And in the depths of the palace, in the cold, stone-walled chambers where only the queen and her closest confidants were allowed, the final pieces of her plan began to fall into place.

The empire was hers for the taking, and nothing—not even the gods themselves—would stand in her way.

CHAPTER 13

The town of Stonehaven, with its bustling markets and towering architecture, was no different from any other settlement the shopkeeper had visited over the centuries. To the untrained eye, he was just another aging merchant, peddling wares in a modest, unassuming shop tucked away in a quiet alley. His grizzled beard, sharp eyes, and slightly hunched posture gave him the appearance of a man who had seen much and expected little from the world.

But appearances were deceiving, and the shopkeeper was far from an ordinary man. He was Aurelius, a spy for the gods, an ageless being tasked with watching over the mortal realm and reporting back to the divine. His true form was that of an immortal observer, bound by the will of the gods to walk among mortals, gather information, and subtly influence events according to their grand design.

Aurelius had been many things over the eons—a scribe, a scholar, a merchant—but always he had been a spy. His task was simple: to watch, to listen, and to report. His loyalty was to the gods, but he was also bound by their laws, forbidden to interfere unless commanded. And so he had honed the art of subtlety, mastering the delicate balance of guiding mortals without them ever knowing they were being guided.

On the morning of the royal announcement, as Queen Selenia wove her web of lies, Aurelius sat in his shop in Stonehaven, sipping a cup of tea and perusing a dusty tome on ancient magic. His shop was quiet, the early hour keeping most customers at bay, but that was precisely how he liked it. It gave him time to think, to plan, and to reflect on the delicate threads of fate that were being woven around the world.

He had been in this town for weeks, ever since he had sensed the shift in the balance of power at the imperial court. The arrival of Zephyros and Elion had not gone unnoticed, nor had their subsequent encounter with the dark elves, Kumori and Iwa. Aurelius had watched from the shadows, careful not to reveal himself, but he had sensed the tension, the uncertainty, and the growing threat that loomed over them all.

The gods were uneasy, that much was clear. They had sent him here for a reason, though they had not revealed all their plans. It was not his place to question, only to observe and to report. But there was something different this time—something that made him wonder if the gods themselves were not as all-knowing as they claimed to be.

Aurelius's thoughts were interrupted by the sound of the bell above his door chiming softly. He looked up to see a young woman entering the shop, her eyes wide with curiosity as she took in the shelves of strange and unusual items. He offered her a polite smile, masking his true thoughts behind the guise of a friendly shopkeeper.

"Good morning," he greeted her, his voice warm and inviting. "What can I help you with today?"

She smiled shyly, glancing around at the various trinkets and oddities that lined the shelves. "I'm just looking, thank you. Your shop is so unique."

Aurelius chuckled, waving dismissively. "Oh, it's nothing special, a collection of odds and ends I've picked up over the years. But if you see anything that catches your eye, don't hesitate to ask."

As the woman browsed, Aurelius's thoughts returned to the events of the previous night. Zephyros and his companions were making their way toward the Shadowed Vale, a place that was both ancient and powerful, a place where the boundaries between the mortal world and the divine were thin. It was no coincidence that the gods had sent him here to this town at this time.

He could sense the threads of fate weaving themselves into a complex pattern, one that would have far-reaching consequences for the entire world. But there were too many variables, too many unknowns for even Aurelius to see the full picture. All he could do was watch and wait and be ready to act when the time came. As the young woman made her purchase and left the shop, Aurelius returned to his tea, his mind already drifting back to the task at hand.

The gods had entrusted him with this mission, and he would not fail them. But there was a growing sense of unease in the back of his mind, a feeling that things were spiraling out of control, that the gods themselves were struggling to keep the balance.

For the first time in centuries, Aurelius wondered if the gods were truly infallible. He had served them faithfully for so long, had followed their commands without question, but the events of recent days had shaken his confidence. The dark forces at play were ancient, older even than the gods themselves, and they were growing stronger with each passing day. As he sat there, lost in thought, Aurelius felt a familiar tingling at the back of his mind—a sign that one of his contacts was reaching out to him. He closed his eyes, focusing on the sensation, and allowed the connection to form.

In his mind's eye, he saw the familiar figure of Celestia, the goddess who had originally tasked him with his mission. She was a being of light and power, her form shifting and changing like a living flame. Her voice echoed in his mind, filled with the authority of one who had watched over the world for millennia.

"Aurelius," she intoned, her voice resonating with divine power, "the time is approaching. You have seen the signs, have you not?"

He nodded, his mental voice calm and composed. "I have, My Lady. The darkness grows stronger, and the mortals you have set on this path are drawing closer to the Vale. But I sense… uncertainty, even among the gods. Is there something you are not telling me?"

There was a pause, and for a moment Aurelius feared he had overstepped his bounds. But then Celestia's voice softened, a note of concern creeping into her tone. "You are perceptive, Aurelius. Indeed, there is much we cannot see, even with our power. The darkness that stirs is ancient, older than us, and it is shrouded in secrecy. We do not know its true nature, nor its full intent."

Aurelius's unease grew. "Then what is my role in this, My Lady? How can I serve if even the gods are uncertain?"

Her form flickered, her light dimming slightly. "Your role is as it has always been—to observe, to gather information, and to guide the mortals as best you can. They are the key to stopping this darkness, but they will need your help to see the path clearly."

Aurelius bowed his head in acknowledgment. "I will do as you command, My Lady. But I must warn you that forces at play here may be beyond even our control. The queen, the creature from the Abyss, and now the movements of the gods themselves... The threads of fate are tangled, and I fear that we may not be able to untangle them in time."

Celestia's light brightened, her voice firm with resolve. "We must try, Aurelius. The fate of the world depends on it. Continue your mission and be vigilant. The time will come when you must act, and when it does, you must be ready."

The connection faded, and Aurelius was once again alone in his shop. He opened his eyes, feeling the weight of the goddess's words settle over him like a heavy cloak. The gods were not omnipotent, not infallible, and they were as uncertain as the mortals they watched over.

Aurelius finished his tea, setting the empty cup aside with a sigh. The time was indeed approaching, and he knew that he would need to be at the top of his game to see this mission through. There was no room for doubt, no room for error. He had to be ready, had to be vigilant, for the fate of the world might well rest on his shoulders.

As the day wore on and the town of Stonehaven bustled with life, Aurelius kept a careful watch, his sharp eyes taking in every detail, every movement. He knew that Zephyros and his companions would return, that they would seek him out again, whether they knew it or not. And when they did, he would be there, ready to guide them down the path the gods had set for them—or perhaps, the path that fate itself had chosen.

For now, Aurelius was content to play his part, blend into the background, and observe. But he knew that the time was coming when he would have to step out of the shadows and into the light, to reveal himself for what he truly was.

The gods were watching, and so was Aurelius.

CHAPTER 14

The city of Elarion was a place of whispers and shadows, where power played out in the quiet corridors of the imperial palace and on the lips of nobles at court. And it was here, amidst the grandiose halls and the bustling streets, that Enilcmai found himself once more drawn back to the capital by a call of duty that had never truly left him.

Enilcmai was a paladin of immense stature, towering over most men, his presence commanding and noble. His armor gleamed in the dim light of the city streets, the mark of his order—a radiant sunburst—emblazoned across his chest plate. His piercing blue eyes, framed by weathered features, missed little, and though his face was lined with age and battle, it was clear that his strength and resolve had not diminished over the years.

He had fought many battles, and not only with his sword and shield. Enilcmai had long served as a beacon of hope and justice, a warrior-priest dedicated to the gods, but more importantly, to the ideals of righteousness and truth. He had stood beside Zephyros in a war long past, a conflict that had nearly torn the land apart. Together, they had weathered the storm, emerging victorious, though the scars of that war—both physical and emotional—still lingered.

But time had passed, and the paths of the two warriors had diverged. While Zephyros had pursued a more shadowed and perilous journey, one fueled by vengeance against the gods themselves, Enilcmai had remained loyal to his oaths, traveling across the lands as a protector of the innocent and a champion of the divine. Now, fate was bringing them back together.

Enilcmai strode through the streets of Elarion, his mind heavy with the recent news he had overheard at the palace. Queen Selenia, standing before the court, had announced that her son, Prince Aethas, had been kidnapped by assassins—dark elves, she had claimed, cruel and heartless killers who had spirited the boy away for reasons unknown.

Her performance had been flawless, her grief palpable, but Enilcmai had felt something off in her words, something that didn't sit right. Perhaps it was his years of service, his countless encounters with lies dressed as truths, but the queen's proclamation had left him unsettled. There was something she wasn't telling them, something dark lurking beneath the surface of her sorrowful façade. And so he had decided to act.

Aethas was the future of the empire, a prince who had shown great promise, and Enilcmai knew that the boy's fate could determine the fate of the entire realm. He could not allow this tragedy to go unanswered, not when the queen herself seemed so eager to manipulate the court's sympathies for her own ends. If the queen would not act in the prince's best interests, then Enilcmai would. The paladin's steps were sure as he waded through the crowded market district. He had made inquiries, spoken to a few trusted contacts, and it seemed that the trail of the assassins—the dark elves—led toward the northern wilderness, beyond the Stonefang Mountains. There, in the shadow of those ancient peaks, was the mysterious Shadowed Vale, a place of legend and danger. It was said that only the most daring—or the most foolish—ventured there, and fewer still returned.

But Enilcmai was no stranger to danger. He had faced worse odds before, and if that was where the assassins had taken the prince, then that was where he would go. As he exited the bustling marketplace, his eyes caught sight of a familiar landmark—an old stone tavern that had stood in Elarion for as long as he could remember. A strange tug of memory pulled at him, and he paused, frowning slightly. It was here, long ago, that he had first crossed paths with Zephyros.

The thought of the wizard brought a wave of nostalgia and a touch of sadness. Zephyros had been a comrade, a friend, but after the war, he had changed. The pain of losing his family had twisted him, driving him down a path of vengeance against the very gods Enilcmai served.

The last time they had spoken, it had not ended well. Zephyros had been consumed by his desire for revenge, his heart darkened by grief, and Enilcmai had feared for his friend's soul. Still, despite their differences, Enilcmai had never forgotten Zephyros. In many ways, the wizard had been like a brother to him, and though their paths had diverged, Enilcmai had always hoped that one day they might find a way to reconcile. But that day was not today. Today, his focus was on the prince—and on finding the assassins who had taken him.

As Enilcmai continued on, a strange sense of fate settled over him, as if the gods themselves were guiding his steps. The road ahead would be long and dangerous, but he was ready. Whatever was in the Shadowed Vale, he would face it with the strength of his faith and the steel of his sword.

* * *

Zephyros and Elion continued their journey through the winding, shadowed paths that led deeper into the northern wilds. The forest around them had grown darker, the trees taller and more twisted, their branches reaching out like skeletal fingers that clawed at the sky.

Zephyros had been quiet for much of the journey, his mind occupied by the revelations of the past days. The gods were watching them, he knew that much, but what troubled him more was the sense that something else—something far older and darker—was lurking in the shadows.

He could feel it in the air, a presence that seemed to whisper on the wind, its voice soft but insistent. Elion, sensing his friend's unease, finally broke the silence. "You've been awfully quiet, Zephyros. Something on your mind?"

Zephyros glanced at Elion, his expression grim. "There's something wrong here. I can feel it. The gods are watching us, but it's more than that. There's something…ancient out there, something dark."

Elion frowned, his hand resting on the hilt of his sword. "You think it's connected to the assassins or to the prince?"

"I don't know. But whatever it is, we'll have to face it soon. I can feel it getting closer."

Before Elion could respond, they both froze, their senses suddenly alert. Someone was coming—someone powerful. From the shadows of the trees, a figure emerged, tall and armored, his presence commanding and unmistakable. It took Zephyros only a moment to recognize him, and when he did, his eyes widened in surprise.

"Enilcmai," Zephyros said, his voice filled with both disbelief and recognition.

The paladin stopped a few paces away, his gaze fixed on Zephyros. "It's been a long time, Zephyros."

He felt a strange mix of emotions—surprise, nostalgia, and a touch of sadness. "Too long. What brings you here?"

Enilcmai grimaced. "I'm looking for the prince—and the assassins who took him. I overheard Queen Selenia's announcement. If Aethas is in danger, then I can't sit idly by. I have to find him."

Zephyros exchanged a glance with Elion, his mind racing. The last thing they had expected was to cross paths with Enilcmai again, especially in a place like this. And yet here he was, as resolute and righteous as ever.

For a moment, there was silence, the weight of their shared past hanging in the air between them.

"We're looking for him too, but there's more to this than the queen is letting on. The assassins—Kumori and Iwa—they're not the real threat. The queen is hiding something, something dark," Zephyros said.

Zephyros took a deep breath, the thick, heavy air of the Shadowed Vale clinging to his lungs. This was no mere reunion between old comrades; the eerie silence that surrounded them hinted at deeper currents of fate at play. The towering trees swayed gently, their branches casting strange, shifting shadows on the ground. The atmosphere was oppressive, as if the very air itself held secrets too dark to be spoken aloud.

Elion shifted uneasily, his eyes scanning the mist-laden landscape, while Enilcmai remained still, his expression unreadable. None of them spoke at first, the weight of unspoken words hanging between them. Zephyros glanced from one to the other, the tension palpable. He could sense that each of them had their own questions, their own uncertainties about what lay ahead—and about each other.

At last, Zephyros broke the silence, his voice quiet but firm. "It's been a long time, Enilcmai. We've all changed. The path we're walking now… it's different from the battles we fought before."

Enilcmai met his gaze, the gleam of his armor dim in the waning light. "Different, yes. But we've always walked the edge of darkness, Zephyros. You know that as well as I do." He paused, his tone softening slightly. "But I sense more than just darkness in this Vale. There are forces at play we cannot see. If we're to face them, we need to trust each other. Completely."

Elion's brow furrowed, his hand resting on the hilt of his sword. "Trust doesn't come easily," he said, his voice low. "Not after everything we've been through. But you're right. We have no choice but to rely on each other if we're going to make it through this."

Zephyros nodded, the knot of tension in his chest loosening just a fraction. They weren't fully united yet, but the veil of uncertainty between them had begun to lift. He took a step closer to his old comrades, the shadows of the Vale closing in around them like the coming storm.

"We speak tonight," he said, his eyes narrowing. "No more secrets. We need to understand where each of us stands if we're to survive what's coming."

For a moment, silence reigned again, but this time it was different—less heavy, less uncertain. Enilcmai gave a single nod, and Elion, though hesitant, agreed as well.

And so, with the past unresolved and the future looming before them like an uncharted Abyss, the three companions stood united once more. The eerie shadows of the Vale seemed to twist and writhe around them, as if the very landscape was watching, waiting. Together, they would step into the unknown, where the fate of the prince—and perhaps the entire world—rested uneasily in their hands.

CHAPTER 15

The clearing is a strange, eerie place that felt as though it existed outside of time itself. The trees surrounding it stood impossibly tall, their trunks gnarled and ancient, their twisted branches forming a tangled canopy overhead. Light barely penetrated here, casting long shadows across the ground. The air was thick with the scent of damp earth and old magic, the very essence of the Vale pulsing beneath their feet.

It was wide and circular, its center dominated by a large stone archway, its surface etched with glowing, ancient runes that shimmered faintly in the dim light. The ground was smooth, almost unnaturally so, as if the space had been carefully crafted rather than formed by nature. Moss-covered stones lined the outer edge of the clearing, and the faint sound of water could be heard trickling from somewhere nearby, though the source was hidden in the shadows.

"This is it," Zephyros said quietly, his eyes fixed on the stone arch. "The entrance to the heart of the Vale."

Elion and Enilcmai moved cautiously around him, their gazes sweeping the area. Elion's hand rested lightly on the hilt of his sword, ready for any danger, while Enilcmai's paladin senses were alive with the presence of something unseen. The magic here was thick, almost suffocating, and both men felt its weight pressing down on them. The atmosphere buzzed with a hum of energy, as if the Vale itself were watching their every move.

The faint glow of the runes intensified as they neared the arch, responding to their presence. Zephyros could feel the magic tugging at him, beckoning them forward. But before they could take another step, a ripple of movement caught Elion's eye—a shadow shifting just at the edge of the clearing.

"We're not alone," Elion muttered, his voice barely a whisper.

From the shadows, figures began to emerge—silent and deadly. Clad in dark cloaks that blended with the gloom, they moved with lethal precision, their faces hidden behind masks that reflected no light. Five assassins, their gleaming blades at the ready, slowly encircled the group, their movements precise, almost mechanical.

Enilcmai stepped forward, his war hammer held firmly in his grip. "Stay sharp," he said quietly, his voice filled with the calm confidence of a man who had faced danger many times before.

Zephyros glanced around at the masked figures, his mind racing. The entrance to the Shadowed Vale lay just ahead, but first, they would have to face whatever test these assassins had prepared for them.

One of the assassins, a tall figure with a curved blade, said, "You should not have come here, outsiders. The Vale is not for the likes of you."

Elion stepped forward, his hand tightening around the hilt of his sword. "We don't want trouble. We're here to speak with Varun."

The assassin tilted his head, his voice cold. "Varun does not meet with trespassers. Leave now or face the consequences."

Zephyros narrowed his eyes. "We're not leaving." The assassin said nothing more, simply raising his hand in a swift motion, signaling the attack. In an instant, the assassins moved, their blades flashing in the dim light as they rushed toward the three men.

Elion was the first to react, his sword sliding from its sheath in one fluid motion. He parried the first strike with a ring of steel, his blade dancing as he countered the assassin's swift attacks. His movements were graceful, almost effortless, as he deflected blow after blow, his years of training as a warrior evident in every motion.

Zephyros, meanwhile, summoned the power of the storm. With a flick of his wrist, he unleashed a bolt of lightning that crackled through the air, striking one of the assassins and sending him crashing to the ground, his body convulsing from the electric shock. Another assassin came at him from the side, but Zephyros reacted quickly, calling upon the winds to whip around him, creating a barrier of swirling air that deflected the attack.

Enilcmai stood firm at the center of the group. As one of the assassins lunged toward him, the paladin raised his shield with a powerful sweep, deflecting the strike with ease. His war hammer swung in a wide arc, the force behind it enough to shatter stone. It connected with the assassin's chest, sending him flying back with a sickening crunch.

"Enough!" a voice boomed through the clearing, its power undeniable. The assassins froze in place, their eyes widening in shock as a figure emerged from the shadows. Varun, the leader of the Shadowed Vale, stepped forward, his dark robes billowing around him. His eyes, glowing faintly with the ancient magic of the Vale, swept over the scene before landing on Zephyros and his companions.

"You dare bring violence into the Vale?" Varun's voice was cold, his gaze sharp. Zephyros straightened, lowering his hand as the winds around him died down.

"We had no choice. Your assassins attacked first."

Varun's eyes flicked to the assassins, who quickly lowered their weapons and stepped back, their faces hidden behind their masks. He turned back to Zephyros, his expression unreadable. "What business do you have in the Vale?"

"We seek answers," Zephyros replied. "Answers about the darkness spreading across the empire. We need your help, Varun."

Before Varun could respond, there was a rustling in the underbrush behind them. All eyes turned to see three figures emerging from the trees—Kumori, Iwa, and Prince Aethas. The dark elves moved with practiced stealth, their eyes scanning the scene with caution. Kumori's gaze settled on Varun, and he stepped forward, his expression respectful but serious.

"We came seeking your guidance, Varun. The prince needs your help." Varun's eyes shifted from Zephyros to Kumori and then to Aethas. For a moment, there was silence, the tension in the air thick and palpable. But then, slowly, Varun nodded.

"Very well," he said. "You have all come seeking answers, and you shall have them. But not here. Come with me."

He turned and began walking toward the archway. The assassins sheathed their blades and moved to follow, though their eyes remained wary of the outsiders.

Zephyros, Elion, Enilcmai, Kumori, Iwa, and Aethas exchanged glances, the tension between them still unresolved. But they knew that for now their goals aligned and that they would have to set aside their differences to uncover the truth behind the darkness that threatened the empire. Together, they followed Varun through the narrow opening in the rock, descending into the hidden depths of the Shadowed Vale.

The meeting room was carved from stone, its walls etched with ancient runes that glowed faintly in the dim light. A large circular table stood at the center of the room, surrounded by chairs made of dark wood. The air was cool, the scent of earth and moss heavy in the air. Varun stood at the head of the table, his hands resting on its surface as he regarded the assembled group with a piercing gaze.

"You have come to the Vale seeking answers," Varun began, his voice steady. "But you must understand this place is not a sanctuary for the weak or the unworthy. The magic of the Vale is ancient, and it does not suffer fools lightly."

Zephyros met Varun's gaze. "We didn't come here lightly. The darkness spreading through the empire is connected to something ancient, something from the Abyss. We need to know what we're dealing with."

Varun's eyes flicked to Aethas, who sat quietly beside Kumori and Iwa. "And you, young prince? What do you seek?"

Aethas straightened, his voice steady despite the weight of his words. "I seek to save my father—and the empire—from whatever force has corrupted him. If the Vale holds the answers, then I will do whatever it takes to find them."

Varun regarded the prince for a long moment before nodding. "Very well. But know this—what you seek will not come easily. The path ahead is fraught with danger, and the choices you make here will determine the fate of not only the empire, but the world."

Each member of the group felt the gravity of the situation pressing down on them.

For Zephyros, Elion, Kumori, Iwa, Aethas, and Enilcmai, the road ahead would demand more than their strength. It would demand their trust in one another and their ability to face the darkness.

CHAPTER 16

The air in the chamber was thick with tension as Varun stood before the group, his gaze steady and his voice calm. The ancient magic of the Shadowed Vale hummed softly in the background, a reminder of the power that surrounded them. The room was dimly lit, with the faint glow of runes etched into the stone walls casting shadows across the faces of Zephyros, El-ion, Kumori, Iwa, Aethas, and Enilcmai.

"You all know why you've come here," Varun began, his voice resonating with the weight of his knowledge. "The Abyss is not just a place—it is a prison, a realm where dark forces have been locked away since the dawn of time. To enter it, to face the darkness within, requires a weapon of great power. And that weapon is the key to both unlocking the Abyss and defeating the evil that resides there."

The group listened intently.

"This weapon is no ordinary blade," Varun continued. "It was forged by the gods themselves, split into two pieces and hidden across the land to prevent it from ever being fully wielded by mortals. The hilt and the blade were separated, placed in locations where few would dare venture."

Zephyros leaned forward, his eyes sharp. "Where are these pieces now?"

Varun's gaze turned to Zephyros, his expression unreadable. "The blade lies in the ancient fortress of Kar'Thul, deep in the western wastelands. It is a place of death and decay, haunted by the spirits of those who once ruled there. The blade has been lost for centuries, but it remains protected by those same spirits, and only the worthy can retrieve it."

Kumori's eyes gleamed with determination. "And the hilt?"

"The hilt," Varun said, "is located in the Frozen Peaks, an ancient mountain range far to the east, where the cold is eternal and the paths are treacherous. There, in the heart of the mountain, lies the Temple of Forgotten Kings. The hilt rests within the temple, guarded by forces older than the gods themselves."

Elion frowned, considering the vast distance between the two locations. "We'll need to split up."

Varun nodded. "You will. The blade and the hilt must be reunited to forge the weapon anew. Only then will you be able to enter the Abyss and face the darkness that threatens this world."

Aethas, who had been silent for most of the conversation, finally spoke up. "What about me? Shouldn't I be helping to retrieve one of the pieces?"

Enilcmai, ever the wise paladin, placed a hand on the prince's shoulder. "You will help, Aethas, but for now your strength lies in preparation. The journey ahead will be perilous, and you must be ready to face it. I will stay behind with you, and together we'll train. You need to learn to harness your potential if you're to play a role in this battle."

Aethas, though clearly frustrated, nodded in understanding. He knew that Enilcmai was right—he wasn't ready yet. But with the paladin's guidance, he would become strong enough to aid his companions when the time came.

Varun crossed his arms, his gaze sweeping across the group. "You have your tasks before you. Zephyros,

Elion—you will travel east to the Frozen Peaks to retrieve the hilt. Kumori, Iwa—you will head west to Kar'Thul to retrieve the blade. Time is of the essence, and the longer the weapon remains separated, the stronger the darkness grows."

Kumori and Iwa exchanged a glance, their shared determination evident in the set of their jaws. "We'll find the blade," Kumori said, his voice full of resolve. "Whatever stands in our way, we'll overcome it."

Zephyros nodded, his mind already racing with thoughts of the journey ahead. "We'll get the hilt. And when we reunite the pieces, we'll be ready to enter the Abyss."

Varun inclined his head, a faint smile tugging at the corner of his lips. "I have no doubt that you will. But the path ahead is fraught with danger. You will face trials, both physical and spiritual, that will test the very core of who you are. Stay true to your purpose, and you may yet succeed."

The room fell silent as Varun's words sank in. Each member of the group understood that the fate of the world rested on their shoulders, and that their journey would push them to their limits. Finally, Varun gestured toward the door that led back to the main hall.

"For now, rest. Gather your strength. You will need it in the days to come."

That evening, the group gathered in the great hall of the Shadowed Vale for a meal, the atmosphere heavy with the weight of the mission ahead. The flickering light of the fire cast long shadows on the stone walls, and the scent of roasted meat and fresh bread filled the air. Despite the tension, there was a sense of camaraderie among the group. They had faced much together already, and though they would soon be splitting up, they knew that their bond would remain strong.

Zephyros and Elion sat at one end of the table, discussing their upcoming journey to the Frozen Peaks. "The cold will be brutal," Elion remarked, tearing a piece of bread from a loaf. "But we've faced worse."

"The hilt is the key. If we can get our hands on it, we'll be one step closer to the Abyss," Zephyros said.

Across the table, Kumori and Iwa were quietly discussing their own plans. The western wastelands were a dangerous place, filled with the remnants of ancient wars and haunted by restless spirits. But Kumori was confident that they could retrieve the blade.

"The spirits will test us," Iwa said, his deep voice rumbling like distant thunder.

Kumori smirked, his eyes gleaming. "We've never backed down from a fight. This won't be any different."

Aethas, sitting beside Enilcmai, listened to the conversations around him with a mixture of anticipation and frustration. He wanted to be out there, fighting alongside his companions, but he understood that he still had much to learn. Enilcmai had promised to train him, to teach him the ways of the paladins, and Aethas knew that this was his path for now.

"You'll be ready when the time comes," Enilcmai said quietly, sensing the prince's thoughts. "For now, focus on what you can control, your training and your strength. The rest will follow."

Aethas nodded, feeling the weight of the paladin's words settle over him like a cloak. "I won't let you down." As the meal came to an end, the group exchanged quiet farewells. The next morning, they would set out on their separate journeys—Kumori and Iwa to the west, Zephyros and Elion to the east. Aethas and Enilcmai would remain behind, preparing for the battle to come.

The night was quiet as the group retreated to their rooms, each of them lost in their own thoughts. Outside, the Vale was still, the ancient magic of the land humming softly in the background. Tomorrow, the real journey would begin, and the fate of the world would hang in the balance.

CHAPTER 17

The grand chambers of Queen Selenia were cloaked in darkness, lit only by the flickering glow of enchanted candles. The long shadows cast by the faint light danced along the marble walls, adding to the ominous atmosphere that had taken hold of the imperial palace since the announcement of Prince Aethas's death.

Selenia, seated on her ornate throne, appeared every bit the grieving mother—her hands clasped tightly on her lap, her expression cold and distant. But those who knew the queen's true nature understood that behind her mask of sorrow was a calculating mind, twisting the fate of the empire to her will.

She heard a quiet knock at the chamber door, and with a flick of her wrist, the massive wooden door creaked open. A hooded figure stepped inside—a spy, one of the many who served her across the empire, gathering information and whispering secrets into her ear.

The spy knelt before her, his face hidden beneath the shadows of his cloak. "My Queen," he said, his voice trembling slightly, "I bring news."

She regarded him coolly, her fingers tapping the armrest of her throne. "Speak."

"Zephyros, Elion, and another—a paladin—have entered the Shadowed Vale."

The queen's eyes narrowed, and for a moment, her calm façade flickered. She knew Zephyros was a threat, but the addition of a paladin—likely Enilcmai, one of the most revered and powerful warriors of his kind—complicated things. They were heading into the Shadowed Vale, where she could not directly interfere, at least not without exposing her alliances with darker forces. But there were ways to act, and Selenia was never one to leave loose ends unchecked.

Behind her, in the darkest corner of the room, the figure of her dark companion stirred—the sorcerer with glowing purple eyes who had been guiding her since her alliance with the forces of the Abyss.

He stepped forward, his voice a soft hiss. "They must be stopped before they gather what they seek," the sorcerer murmured. "The Vale holds too many secrets. If they obtain the weapon, it could spell disaster for our plans."

Selenia's lips curved into a thin smile, her mind already plotting her next move. "Then we will stop them," she said smoothly. "But not directly. Not yet." The sorcerer's glowing eyes watched her closely, awaiting her decision. "We have an advantage," Selenia continued. "Kumori and Iwa are dark elves, and like calls to like. They can be influenced, delayed, perhaps even manipulated. If we can target them first, the others will be slowed."

The queen rose gracefully from her throne, her gown flowing behind her like liquid night. "Summon Selhara." The spy flinched slightly at the name but quickly obeyed, disappearing from the chamber without a word.

Moments later, a new presence filled the room—a tall, lithe figure with dark skin and piercing silver eyes. Selhara, a dark elf assassin and mage, entered with the grace of a shadow slipping through the night. She wore black leather armor that hugged her form, with twin daggers strapped to her hips and a staff of gnarled wood on her back. Her long, white hair fell in a sleek braid down her back, and her expression was one of quiet confidence, tempered by the dangerous power she carried.

"You summoned me, My Queen," Selhara said, her voice a low, sultry purr.

Selenia's eyes flicked over the assassin, approving of the strength and cunning Selhara exuded. "Yes, Selhara, I have a task for you."

"I am at your service," Selhara replied, though the faintest hint of a smirk tugged at her lips. It was well known among those who served the queen that Selhara took orders, but only as long as they aligned with her own interests.

Selenia stepped forward, her expression darkening. "Zephyros, Elion, and the paladin are in the Shadowed Vale. I want you to follow them, find out what they are after, and delay them. Focus on the two dark elves with them, Kumori and Iwa. They will be more easily influenced."

Selhara's silver eyes gleamed with interest. "Kumori and Iwa, I've heard of them. Talented, from what I gather."

"Talented, yes," Selenia agreed, "but no one is beyond manipulation. Find them, gather information, and report back to me. If necessary, intervene. But be careful. The Vale is dangerous, and Varun will not allow outsiders to meddle with its secrets."

Selhara inclined her head, a faint smile playing on her lips. "Understood, My Queen. Consider it done."

Selenia nodded, satisfied. "Good. There's a town near the entrance to the Vale, Stonehaven. Start there. Discreetly learn where they've been, where they're headed, and report back." With a final nod, Selhara turned and disappeared into the shadows, leaving the queen alone with her dark companion.

The sorcerer stepped closer, his eyes gleaming with approval. "She is a strong choice. She will find them."

"She must," Selenia said quietly. "If Zephyros and his group succeed in their mission, everything we have built will be in jeopardy. The weapon must remain divided."

* * *

Selhara moved through the crowded streets of Stonehaven with practiced ease, her presence unnoticed by the busy townsfolk. The dwarven city, carved into the mountainside, was alive with the sound of metal clanging and merchants calling out to passersby. Despite the bustling activity, the dark elf assassin moved like a shadow, slipping from one alley to the next, gathering information from the whispers of the town.

Her first stop had been a small tavern near the city gates. She had overheard a few locals discussing a group of travelers—one of whom had white hair and carried a sword of lightning. Kumori. He and Iwa had passed through recently, along with a few others, though no one knew where they were headed exactly. Her second stop had been a blacksmith's forge, where she learned of a cart with strange, rune-covered supplies that had been purchased by a tall elf with glowing hands—Elion, undoubtedly. The blacksmith had mentioned that the group had asked about maps to the wilderness, specifically mentioning the Vale.

Satisfied with the intel she had gathered, Selhara paused at the edge of town, gazing out toward the dense forest that led to the Shadowed Vale. Her silver eyes glinted in the dying light of the day as she considered her next move. She had enough information to track them now, and soon she would find them within the Vale.

But Selhara was patient. She would bide her time, learn more, and only strike when the moment was right. Kumori and Iwa intrigued her—they were powerful in their own right, but they were also dark elves like herself. And in the end, she believed that even the strongest could be swayed if given the right reason. As the sun dipped below the horizon and the shadows deepened, Selhara smiled to herself. The hunt had begun.

CHAPTER 18

Selhara moved swiftly through the twilight streets of Stonehaven, her form blending into the fading shadows as night fell. The information she had gathered was enough to track down Zephyros, Elion, Kumori, and the others. Soon, she would find them and delay their progress in the Shadowed Vale. Her mission was clear, and her queen's orders rang in her ears like a steady drumbeat. As she approached the edge of town, the mountains looming overhead, she felt the familiar excitement of the hunt building within her.

She glanced around to make sure no one was watching, her steps light and silent as she prepared to leave the town behind.

"Leaving so soon, are we?" came a voice from the darkness.

Selhara's body froze in an instant, her hand reflexively moving to the hilt of her dagger as her silver eyes scanned the surrounding shadows. It was nearly impossible for anyone to catch her off guard, especially not when she was in her element. But this voice carried a strange weight, an unsettling knowingness. It shouldn't have been possible for anyone to see her. Not here. Not like this.

A figure stepped from the shadows—an older man with a grizzled beard and sharp eyes, dressed in simple merchant's garb. Selhara recognized him instantly. The unremarkable shopkeeper. Aurelius. She'd heard of him before but paid him little mind. A harmless, small-town fixture. Or so she thought.

Selhara narrowed her eyes, ready for anything. "And who might you be, old man, to sneak up on someone like me?"

Aurelius gave her a knowing smile, one that carried no fear of the dark elf assassin standing before him. "Oh, I'm someone who knows a little more than most. And I thought it was time we had a chat." Before Selhara could react, Aurelius flicked his hand, and the world around them shifted, the edges of reality warping and twisting. In the blink of an eye, the bustling streets of Stonehaven vanished, and the two of them stood in a wide, open space—an ancient stone courtyard, surrounded by tall, weathered walls. The air crackled with latent magic, and the dim light of twilight had given way to a strange, ethereal glow.

Selhara's eyes widened in surprise, and she immediately drew her daggers, her muscles tensing for a fight. "What is this? How did you—"

Aurelius simply raised his hand, stopping her mid-sentence. "No need for hostilities, Selhara. I brought us here to talk. But I'm more than happy to demonstrate if you want to see what I'm capable of."

Selhara, though taken aback by his power, wasn't one to be easily intimidated. She twirled her daggers in her hands, the silver blades glinting in the strange light.

"You can transport me to this place, but that doesn't mean you're my equal. I'm no common assassin."

Aurelius chuckled softly, his eyes glinting with a knowledge far deeper than his appearance suggested. "Oh, I'm well aware of that. You're Selhara, the dark elf assassin who serves Queen Selenia. Powerful, cunning, and skilled with both blade and magic. But you see, I'm no common shopkeeper either."

His form began to shift. His grizzled appearance melted away, revealing his true form—a tall, ageless figure cloaked in a shimmering robe that seemed to ripple with the power of the gods. His eyes, now glowing with an intense light, bore into Selhara's soul. The ground beneath their feet seemed to tremble slightly as his magic surged.

Selhara took a cautious step back, her daggers still at the ready. "Who are you?"

"I am Aurelius, a servant of the gods. I watch, I listen, and I act when necessary," he said, his voice resonating with power. "And right now, I'm here to make you an offer. We're both spies, you and I. But we serve different masters. I serve the gods, while you serve Selenia and her dark forces. Our paths have crossed, and now we must decide—do we work against each other, or can we find common ground?"

Selhara frowned, her grip on her daggers tightening. She wasn't one to trust easily, especially not someone who claimed to serve the gods. But there was something about Aurelius that made her hesitate.

"What do you want from me?"

Aurelius spread his hands in a gesture of peace. "I don't want to stop you from doing your queen's bidding, but I believe our goals may align—at least for now. The forces at play are larger than either of us. If you fail to delay Zephyros and his group, they will still press on, and you will have gained nothing. But together we might be able to slow them down, learn more about their plans, and buy ourselves some time to shape the outcome."

Selhara's eyes narrowed. "You think you can manipulate me?"

"No," Aurelius said, his voice calm but firm. "I think we can help each other. You don't trust me. I know that. But I also know you're not blind to the bigger picture. The gods, the Abyss, the weapons that Zephyros and his friends seek—they're part of something much larger than you realize. I'm offering you a chance to be part of it. To understand it."

Selhara didn't like being in the dark, and though she had her own agenda, there was something tantalizing about the idea of working alongside someone with such deep knowledge of the gods and their plans. "And if I refuse?"

Aurelius smiled faintly. "Then you'll do what you always do—strike from the shadows and hope it's enough. But you won't have my knowledge to guide you."

She weighed her options. The power Aurelius had shown her was undeniable. Perhaps he could be useful—for now.

"Very well," Selhara said, lowering her daggers slightly. "We can work together, but I have my own interests to protect, and I won't hesitate to act if I think you're trying to play me." Aurelius inclined his head, his smile widening. "Of course. I wouldn't expect anything less."

The air between them seemed to shift once more, and in an instant the stone courtyard dissolved, replaced by the familiar streets of Stonehaven. The town was quiet now, the night fully descended, and the shadows longer than before. Selhara blinked, finding herself standing exactly where she had been before Aurelius had intervened. But now there was no sign of the mysterious spy for the gods. He had vanished, leaving her to contemplate their strange encounter.

For a long moment, Selhara stood still, her thoughts swirling as she replayed the conversation in her mind. She didn't trust Aurelius, but she knew that the information he offered was valuable. And for now, that was enough. With a deep breath, Selhara adjusted the straps of her weapons and continued on her path out of town.

The hunt for Zephyros and his companions was far from over, and now she had more than one reason to find them. As she disappeared into the night, the streets of Stonehaven fell silent once more, unaware of the strange alliances and dark forces that were converging around them.

CHAPTER 19

Aurelius stood in the Ether's stillness, a realm beyond the mortal plane where only gods and their chosen emissaries could tread. The air shimmered with light that seemed to come from nowhere and everywhere all at once, casting soft hues across the endless expanse. Before him, the thrones of the gods loomed, each one occupied by a being of unfathomable power and radiance.

The gods of this realm, beings that governed the balance of life and death, watched the mortal world with great interest, manipulating fate and destiny to maintain their cosmic order. Aurelius, the ever-watchful servant, knelt before them in deference, awaiting their judgment.

One of the gods, a figure cloaked in golden light, spoke first. It was Celestia, goddess of light and order, her voice a clear chime in the ethereal void. "Aurelius, you have served us well thus far, but your latest report troubles us."

Aurelius kept his eyes lowered, speaking in measured tones. "My Lords, the situation has become more complex. I encountered Selhara, the queen's assassin. She seeks to delay Zephyros and his companions in their quest for the sword. I have offered her cooperation, though her loyalties remain…flexible."

There was a murmur among the gods, a shifting of power as they communicated silently.

Malkor, the god of death and secrets, his voice a deep, resonant echo, spoke, "And what of the paladin, Enilcmai? He is with them now."

At the mention of Enilcmai, the air in the ether grew colder. Aurelius had anticipated this reaction. The gods had known Enilcmai for centuries, respected him for his strength and virtue but also feared him for the same reasons. His presence complicated everything.

"Yes," Aurelius replied carefully. "He has joined their group. His loyalty to Zephyros is strong, and his power has only grown since you last crossed paths. His presence makes their success more likely." There was a collective shift among the thrones, the gods stirring uneasily.

Even Celestia's radiant form dimmed slightly as she spoke, "Enilcmai is a threat. His faith and strength are unshakable. If he remains with Zephyros, they will succeed in their quest, and the balance we have maintained for so long will be shattered."

Aurelius felt the weight of their displeasure pressing down on him like a heavy mantle. His role had always been to observe, guide subtly, and report. But now the gods were asking for more.

Malkor leaned forward, his voice like a cold wind. "You must ensure that Enilcmai does not succeed. Zephyros and his group must be delayed, diverted. The Abyss cannot be opened, not by their hands. And Enilcmai…he must be dealt with."

Aurelius lifted his head slightly, though he remained kneeling. "What would you have me do, My Lords?" The gods deliberated among themselves, their voices a cacophony of light and shadow.

Celestia shimmered before speaking, "You will wait for Zephyros and his companions at the edge of the Shadowed Vale. When they emerge, you will steer them off the path they were meant to take. Lead them into danger, a place where even their strength may falter. They must not reach the hilt of the sword."

Malkor's shadow deepened, his eyes gleaming with dark intent. "There is a place, the Vale of the Fallen, a cursed land where the dead do not rest. The path is perilous, the creatures there ancient and dangerous. If they venture there, their chances of survival are slim."

Celestia nodded. "The Vale of the Fallen is an appropriate choice. Lead them there, Aurelius. Let them believe it is the way to the hilt, and when they are lost, we will decide how best to remove them from the equation."

Aurelius's mind raced, calculating the risks and rewards. Leading Zephyros into the Vale of the Fallen would indeed slow them down, perhaps even kill some of them. But it was a dangerous game—Zephyros, Elion, Kumori, and especially Enilcmai were not easily deceived. And there was always the possibility that they could survive. Still, the gods had spoken, and Aurelius was bound by their will.

"As you command, My Lords," Aurelius said, bowing his head once more.

Celestia's light flared brighter for a moment. "Do not fail us, Aurelius. The fate of the world rests on maintaining the balance. If Zephyros succeeds, the darkness of the Abyss will spread unchecked, and even we may not be able to contain it."

Malkor's shadow rippled ominously. "Do what must be done. And remember, you serve the gods. Not mortals." The gods' presence began to fade, their forms dissolving into the ether as they returned to their divine realms. Aurelius remained kneeling, the weight of their orders settling heavily on his shoulders. He was bound to their will, yet he could not help but feel the burden of the task they had given him.

Once the gods were gone, Aurelius stood, his form returning to the grizzled, unassuming appearance he usually wore among mortals. He sighed softly, knowing what was ahead. Zephyros, Elion, Enilcmai, Kumori, and Iwa were strong, determined, and guided by a higher purpose. Diverting them would not be easy. But it had to be done. With a flick of his wrist, he opened a portal back to the mortal world, stepping through and emerging near the edge of the Shadowed Vale. The ancient forest was dense and foreboding, its magic pulsing through the air like a heartbeat.

He would wait here, hidden in the shadows, until Zephyros and his companions emerged. Then he would guide them down the wrong path, toward the Vale of the Fallen. It was a place where even Enilcmai's great strength might not save them.

As he prepared for the inevitable encounter, Aurelius could only hope that the gods 'plan would succeed. For if it didn't, the consequences would be dire—for both the mortal world and the gods themselves.

CHAPTER 20

The morning sun filtered through the canopy of the Shadowed Vale, casting soft rays of light across the training grounds where Enilcmai stood with Aethas. The air was crisp and cool, but tension filled the space as Aethas braced himself for another round of training with the seasoned paladin.

The others—Zephyros, Elion, Kumori, and Iwa—were preparing for their separate journeys to recover the pieces of the sword, but for now, all attention was on Aethas. He had proven himself capable, but he was still young, still unpolished. Today, that would change.

Enilcmai crossed his arms, watching as Aethas gripped a massive war hammer, the weapon nearly as long as the young prince was tall. The weight of the hammer made Aethas's arms shake as he lifted it.

"Swing it!" Enilcmai commanded. With a grunt, Aethas swung the hammer in a wide arc, but the momentum carried him too far, his balance faltering as the weapon dragged him forward. He barely managed to avoid falling to the ground, and the hammer landed with a dull thud, far from its intended mark.

Enilcmai shook his head. "No. The hammer's power lies in control, not brute strength. You're trying to overpower it, but your body doesn't work with it."

Aethas wiped the sweat from his brow, frustration clear in his eyes. He was capable, but nothing about the war hammer felt right in his hands. "What if I'm not suited for this weapon?"

The paladin's gaze softened. "That's exactly what we're trying to find out. Not every warrior is meant to wield a hammer."

After retrieving the hammer, Aethas tried his hand at a sword. This time, the weapon felt more comfortable, the balance easier to manage. He worked through basic strikes and parries under Enilcmai's watchful eye, but there was nothing remarkable about his movements. They were precise, but lacked the fluid grace of a seasoned swordsman.

Enilcmai frowned. "Your form is adequate, but you don't feel the weapon. It's not yours." Aethas nodded, panting from the exertion. He had always been determined, but it was hard not to feel defeated. He knew his strengths were somewhere else, but he couldn't yet see where. Enilcmai handed him a spear. "Let's try this."

Aethas took the spear in his hands, and something changed immediately. The weight felt natural, balanced. The long reach of the spear fit perfectly with his instincts to keep his enemies at a distance, to strike with precision and speed. He spun the weapon experimentally, and it whistled through the air with fluid grace.

"Good," Enilcmai said with a hint of satisfaction. "Try again. Attack me."

Aethas didn't hesitate. He lunged forward, thrusting the spear toward the paladin, who easily parried with his shield. But as the spear connected, something unexpected happened. Aethas felt a surge of energy course through his body, and the wind itself seemed to respond to his movements. His feet barely touched the ground as he spun around Enilcmai, attacking from new angles with blinding speed.

The young prince was gliding. Enilcmai's eyes widened slightly as he blocked another attack. "You're not just fighting with the spear," he muttered, more to himself than to Aethas. "You're channeling something deeper." Aethas could feel it, too. As he moved, his body felt lighter, as though the air itself was lifting him, carrying him across the battlefield with ease. His movements were no longer forced or awkward—they were seamless, effortless.

As he thrust the spear forward once more, Aethas noticed something else. His hair, usually a deep chestnut, was lifting as if caught in an invisible breeze. His skin tingled, and his eyes glowed a vibrant green that mimicked the color of emeralds, shimmering with an ethereal light. An aura surrounded him, a faint glow of power that made the air around him hum.

For a moment, even Enilcmai was taken aback. The paladin had faced countless enemies, seen magic in all its forms, but there was something uniquely potent about the way the wind bent to Aethas's will.

"That's enough!" Enilcmai called out, raising his shield and stepping back. Aethas skidded to a halt, panting but exhilarated. The spear lowered, and the glow around him faded, but the energy lingered in the air. He turned to Enilcmai, unsure of what had just happened. The paladin walked over, his expression a mix of surprise and approval. "It seems we've found your weapon."

Aethas looked at the spear in his hand, still catching his breath. "The wind…… I could feel it. It was like it was part of me, guiding me."

Enilcmai nodded. "Wind magic. You've tapped into a power that enhances your combat skills. The spear is your conduit. It allows you to move with the grace and speed of the wind itself. It's rare, but not unheard of. And with practice, you could become a force to be reckoned with."

Aethas felt a sense of pride and determination swell within him. For the first time since their training began, he knew exactly who he was on the battlefield. He wasn't the strongest or the most skilled with brute force, but he didn't need to be. His strength was in his agility, his connection to the wind, and his ability to move faster than his enemies could react.

Nearby, Varun watched the training session with silent contemplation. As a guardian of the Shadowed Vale, he had seen many warriors, many forms of power. But even he could feel the weight of the magic

Aethas had begun to channel. It was ancient, primal, and potent.

The hair on the back of Varun's neck stood up as he observed the shimmering aura around the prince. Whatever power Aethas had tapped into, it was powerful enough to make even a being like Varun take notice. There was something deeply significant about the young man's connection to the wind.

Enilcmai placed a hand on Aethas's shoulder, giving him a firm nod. "We'll continue training, but you've already come far in a short time. You have the potential to become more than you realize, Aethas." The prince smiled, his confidence growing. "Thank you, Enilcmai. I'll be ready."

As the two groups prepared to leave for their separate missions—one heading for the blade, the other for the hilt—Aethas remained behind with Enilcmai. They would continue to train in the Vale, honing Aethas's newfound abilities. The wind, it seemed, had chosen him. And with it, Aethas would carve his own path, not only as a prince but as a warrior worthy of standing beside legends.

CHAPTER 21

The stillness of the Shadowed Vale settled over Varun as he made his way to his private chambers, his steps slow and deliberate. The recent events—the arrival of Zephyros, the reunion of the group with Enilcmai, and the discovery of Aethas's potential—had left a storm of thoughts swirling in his mind. As a guardian of the Vale, he had seen many warriors, many seekers of power, pass through this ancient place, but the convergence of these powerful figures and their intertwined fates weighed heavily on him.

Varun's chambers were carved into the heart of the Vale, their walls covered in ancient runes that pulsed faintly with the magic that coursed through the land. The room was sparse, with little more than a simple bed and a table strewn with scrolls and manuscripts. But Varun preferred it that way. Distractions were unnecessary when one bore the responsibility of protecting the secrets of the Vale.

He lowered himself into a wooden chair, leaning back and closing his eyes, his thoughts racing. The Sword of the Abyss, the ancient weapon that could open the Abyssal Depths and defeat the gods, had always been at the center of his vigilance. But something about this weapon—and the people now involved—felt different.

Aethas.

The boy had potential, more than even Enilcmai or Zephyros realized. His connection to the wind magic, the way his body harmonized with the spear during training—it was more than a coincidence. There was something about the prince that stirred the ancient magic of the Vale, something that even Varun couldn't ignore.

After a few moments of silent reflection, Varun stood, his decision made. There were too many unanswered questions, too many mysteries surrounding the weapon they sought. He needed answers, and there was only one place to find them. The Dark Library.

Hidden deep within the Vale, the Dark Library was a repository of knowledge older than most civilizations. Its tomes and scrolls contained information on the most ancient of magic and the darkest of secrets, many of which even Varun had never dared to read. But now, with so much at stake, he knew it was time to seek out the truth. As he made his way through the narrow corridors of the Vale, the air around him grew colder, the shadows longer. The library was buried deep within the Earth, its entrance a simple stone door marked with symbols of warding, meant to keep those unworthy from entering.

Varun whispered the incantation that unlocked the door, and with a heavy groan, it swung open, revealing the vast chamber beyond. The shelves stretched high into the darkness, each one filled with ancient tomes bound in leather, vellum, and even scales. The air smelled of dust and forgotten power, and the silence was absolute. For the next week, Varun spent nearly every waking moment in the Dark Library, pouring over the texts that referenced the Sword of the Abyss. He found tales of the sword's creation, of the gods who forged it, and the mortals who sought to wield it. But the more he read, the more he began to sense that something was amiss.

The descriptions of the weapon were vague, conflicting even. Some spoke of a sword forged from the essence of the Abyss itself, while others hinted at something far older and more dangerous. Varun combed through scroll after scroll, searching for clarity, until finally, he found what he was looking for. It wasn't a sword.

The truth was buried deep within a manuscript written in a language few mortals could understand. It detailed the creation of the weapon not as a sword but as a spear—a weapon of precision and control, forged to pierce the very fabric of the Abyss and bind its power to the wielder. The manuscript went on to explain that the gods had hidden this truth, disguising the weapon's true form to prevent mortals from ever realizing its full potential.

And then Varun found the most startling revelation of all. The one who wielded the spear would not only open the Abyss, but would also take command of the Abyssal Depths themselves. This wielder would lead the disciples of the Abyss in a war against the gods, with the power to topple even the mightiest of deities.

The spear was the key to overthrowing the gods themselves. Varun's heart pounded in his chest as he reread the passage, the weight of its meaning settling over him like a heavy cloak. Aethas.

The boy was the chosen one. His connection to the spear, his wind magic, his latent power—it all pointed to one conclusion. Aethas was destined to wield the Spear of the Abyss, to lead the disciples of the Abyssal Depths, and to challenge the gods.

For a long moment, Varun sat in the dim light of the library, the revelation swirling in his mind. If the others knew this—if Zephyros, Enilcmai, or even Aethas himself realized what the prince was destined to become—it would change everything. The gods would move against them with even greater force, and their quest would take on a far more dangerous dimension.

Varun closed the manuscript, his decision made. He would keep this information to himself for now. The others were focused on gathering the pieces of the weapon, and that was enough for the time being. But when the time came—when the hilt, the blade, and the shaft of the spear were finally brought together— Varun would be ready. He would be the one to hand the weapon to Aethas, to guide him toward his destiny.

But first, Varun needed to discover how to create the shaft of the spear. It was the one piece of the weapon that was not accounted for, hidden somewhere beyond the reach of any current knowledge. If he could find the key to forging the spear's shaft, he could ensure that when the time came, Aethas would be ready to fulfill his destiny.

With a heavy sigh, Varun stood, the weight of his newfound knowledge pressing down on him. He glanced around the dark library one last time before exiting, sealing the entrance behind him. The others didn't need to know—yet. But the day was coming when the truth would be revealed, and on that day Aethas would either rise as the wielder of the spear or fall beneath the weight of his destiny. And the gods would tremble.

CHAPTER 22

Varun stepped out of the dim, ancient corridors of the dark library, his mind heavy with the revelation he had uncovered. The knowledge that Aethas was the chosen one—the wielder of the spear that could topple the gods—gnawed at him with each step. But for now, that information was his alone to bear. As he made his way through the shadowed paths of the Vale, he decided to check on Aethas and Enilcmai, knowing that the young prince's training was crucial to his future.

The training arena was an open space, surrounded by tall stone walls covered in vines, a place where the assassins of the Vale honed their deadly skills. Today, the sounds of clashing weapons and heavy breathing echoed through the clearing as Aethas trained under Enilcmai's watchful eye. From the shadows, Varun observed.

Aethas moved swiftly, his spear glinting in the soft light of the Vale, the weapon becoming an extension of his will. Enilcmai challenged him with every strike, his heavy shield and war hammer testing the young prince's agility. But it wasn't just Aethas's skill with the spear that caught Varun's attention—it was the wind that danced around him. Every movement seemed to carry with it a breeze, as though the air itself obeyed Aethas's command. But then Varun saw something more.

As Aethas lunged forward, thrusting the spear toward Enilcmai's shield, a faint shimmer enveloped him. The air around Aethas twisted, a subtle distortion, and for the briefest moment Varun saw a flicker of dark-purple light around the prince—so faint that it was barely noticeable, but enough to catch the keen eye of someone who knew what to look for. Varun's heart skipped a beat. The Abyss.

It was there, hidden deep within Aethas, beneath the surface of his power. The dark energy that had always been tied to the Abyss was beginning to awaken within him, but it was still faint, not yet manifesting fully. Enilcmai, focused on Aethas's technique, hadn't noticed it. The paladin was a man of strength and honor, but even he couldn't see what Varun's years of study and experience allowed him to perceive. Aethas unleashed another flurry of attacks, his eyes glowing that familiar emerald green, the wind swirling around him as he moved with uncanny grace. But that purple shimmer returned only for a second before disappearing again into the air.

Is this the true power hidden within him? Varun wondered. *The legacy of the Abyss?*

The thought troubled him. Aethas's potential was undeniable, but if the Abyss had already begun to influence him, then there was far more at stake than simply gathering the pieces of the weapon. Varun had to keep this knowledge hidden for now. Revealing it too soon could disrupt everything. But he also needed answers, and those could not be found within the Shadowed Vale. As the training session continued, Varun turned away from the arena, his thoughts racing. He needed to speak to someone who could help him understand what was happening—someone he trusted.

As he exited the arena, he saw Velkar, his second-in-command, waiting in the shadows nearby. Velkar was a middle-aged elf, his hair streaked with silver, and his piercing eyes glowed faintly in the dim light. A master of the shadow arts, Velkar had long been Varun's most trusted ally. His control over the shadows was unmatched, and his ability to read people made him invaluable as Varun's confidant.

"Velkar," Varun said, his voice calm but edged with urgency, "I need to leave the Vale for a time."

Velkar inclined his head, his expression unreadable. "Where are you headed, My Lord?"

Varun hesitated for a moment before responding. "I'm going to see an old friend. His name is Clerus, one of the most powerful clerics in the world. He rules over the Radiant Plains, far to the east. I believe he may have the answers I seek."

Velkar's brow furrowed slightly. "The Radiant Plains are far from here. What would you ask of Clerus that cannot be found within the Vale?"

Varun's gaze darkened. "There are forces at play beyond even the knowledge stored in our archives. Clerus may know more about the influence of the Abyss and what it could mean for Aethas. But for now, that must remain between us. While I'm gone, I leave the Vale in your care."

Velkar bowed his head in acknowledgment. "You can trust me to keep the Vale safe, My Lord. And to ensure that our guests remain… cooperative."

Varun placed a hand on Velkar's shoulder, appreciating the man's loyalty. "Keep watch over them, especially Aethas. If anything changes with him, I want to know immediately."

"Understood."

Varun turned and left Velkar behind, his cloak billowing as he made his way toward the far edge of the Vale. It had been many years since he had last seen Clerus, but the cleric's wisdom and power were unmatched. Clerus ruled over the Radiant Plains, a land bathed in perpetual sunlight, where the air was warm and the fields stretched as far as the eye could see. The plains were a place of healing and peace, the polar opposite of the shadowed and secretive Vale. Clerus himself was a beacon of light, a towering figure in both stature and power, known for his ability to channel divine magic in ways few could.

The journey would take time, but Varun knew it was necessary. The growing influence of the Abyss over Aethas was a threat, and if left unchecked, it could unravel everything. He needed answers before it was too late. As Varun disappeared into the night, the Shad-owed Vale remained as still and quiet as ever, but the winds were shifting. Far to the east, in the land of light, Clerus would soon receive a visitor. And together, they would decide the fate of the one destined to wield the Spear of the Abyss.

CHAPTER 23

The morning mist lingered over the Shadowed Vale as Zephyros and Elion packed their supplies, their preparations marked by a quiet determination. The Vale's cool air, infused with ancient magic, still hummed faintly around them, but the time had come for them to leave. Their mission to retrieve the hilt of the weapon that would open the Abyss awaited them, and they could not afford any delays.

Elion finished securing the last of their provisions onto the cart, his keen eyes scanning the edge of the Vale. "It feels strange to leave here, knowing what's ahead," he said, his voice quiet but steady. "But we've faced worse."

Zephyros adjusted his cloak, nodding in agreement. "True, but the stakes are higher this time. If we fail, there won't be a second chance."

The two shared a look, their bond as comrades and friends forged in the fires of past battles. They knew the weight of the task before them. Together, they mounted their horses, the majestic creatures stamping the ground with anticipation. With one last glance back at the Vale's towering cliffs and dense forests, they set off. The path out of the Vale was not well-trodden, and as they navigated the winding trails, Zephyros felt a strange tug, an instinct pulling them toward a familiar place.

"Stonehaven," he murmured, glancing at Elion. "Something is pulling us there."

Elion raised an eyebrow, clearly sensing it too. "I suppose we're not done with that place yet."

They altered their course, heading north toward the bustling dwarven city carved into the side of the mountain. Stonehaven's towering gates loomed ahead, and as Zephyros and Elion approached, the familiar clang of hammers and the shouts of merchants filled the air. The city was alive with activity, the streets bustling with traders and craftsmen, their wares on display as dwarves moved in and out of the grand stone structures that lined the market square.

Zephyros's gaze swept the market, and his eyes soon fell on a familiar figure. There, by the side of the road, stood Aurelius, the enigmatic shopkeeper. His cart was set up as usual, filled with various trinkets and supplies that seemed mundane at first glance but carried an air of mystery. The old man's grizzled appearance was the same as before, but Zephyros knew better than to underestimate him. Elion dismounted first, giving Zephyros a sidelong glance.

"The shopkeeper. I didn't expect to see him again."

Zephyros nodded, dismounting as well. "Neither did I. But something tells me this is no coincidence." As they approached Aurelius, the old man greeted them with a knowing smile, his eyes twinkling beneath his weathered brow. "Ah, travelers. It's been a while since we last crossed paths."

Zephyros didn't waste time with pleasantries. "We're heading out on a journey. The hilt of a weapon, hidden far from here."

Aurelius raised an eyebrow, though his expression remained carefully neutral. "Is that so? A dangerous task, no doubt."

Elion stepped closer, his eyes sharp. "You've helped us before. You know things most wouldn't. What do you know of this journey we're on?"

"Ah, well, the world is filled with knowledge, my friends. And some of it falls into the hands of those who can use it. I may not know everything, but I do know that your path will be long and difficult. The hilt you seek lies far from here, in a place where even seasoned travelers like yourselves might struggle to reach."

Zephyros narrowed his eyes. "Where is it?" Aurelius smiled faintly, his eyes gleaming with something deeper than mere amusement.

"To the east, beyond the Frozen Peaks. The hilt is hidden in the Temple of Forgotten Kings, a place guarded by forces older than the gods themselves. The journey there is perilous, and the cold is unforgiving. But it is the path you must take."

Elion frowned, his hand resting on the hilt of his sword. "The Frozen Peaks, that's far from here. And dangerous. What's waiting for us there?"

Aurelius's expression grew more serious. "The temple is a place of great power but also of great trial. Many have sought its treasures, but few have returned.

You'll face more than the cold. The forces guarding the hilt are not of this world."

Zephyros absorbed the information, his mind already calculating the risks and the challenges they would face. The path to the temple would be treacherous, but they had no choice. The hilt was essential, and they had come too far to turn back now.

Aurelius reached into his cart, pulling out a small piece of parchment. "Here. This map will guide you to the edge of the peaks. But once you enter the mountains, you'll be on your own. The way to the temple is not marked by any path that mortals can see."

Elion took the map, studying it briefly before tucking it into his cloak. "Thank you," he said reluctantly. Aurelius nodded, his smile returning.

"You're welcome. Remember, not all who seek the temple return. And even fewer emerge unchanged."

Zephyros gave Aurelius one last look, his suspicions still lingering. There was more to this old man than met the eye, and he couldn't shake the feeling that their meeting here was no accident. But for now, they had the information they needed. Without another word, Zephyros and Elion mounted their horses and set off toward the east, their path now clear. The journey to the Frozen Peaks would be long and grueling, but they were prepared for whatever was ahead. As they rode out of Stonehaven, Zephyros glanced back at the town one last time. Aurelius stood by his cart, watching them leave, his expression unreadable.

The gods had spoken, though not directly. They had guided Aurelius to point them in this direction, leading them toward a path filled with uncertainty and danger. Zephyros knew this, and yet he couldn't deny the pull of destiny driving them forward. The Frozen Peaks awaited. And with them was the hilt of the weapon that could change the fate of the world.

The road stretched out to the horizon, a jagged line where the mountains met the sky. The temperature began to drop as they rode farther east, and the wind grew colder with each passing hour.

Elion broke the silence as they traveled, his breath visible in the crisp air. "Do you trust him? Aurelius?"

Zephyros didn't answer immediately, his gaze fixed ahead. "I don't trust him, but I trust that he knows more than he lets on. And for now that's enough."

The road to the temple would not be an easy one, but Zephyros and Elion had no choice. They would face whatever trials awaited them, because the fate of their world—and perhaps all worlds—rested on the weapon they sought. And as they rode toward the distant mountains, the shadow of the gods loomed ever larger over their journey.

CHAPTER 24

The sun hung low on the horizon as Zephyros and Elion rode through the barren lands east of Stonehaven. The once lively atmosphere of the town now felt like a distant memory, replaced by the cold, desolate air that chilled them to the bone. The road ahead was rough and uneven, twisting and winding through valleys and ridges as the terrain became more treacherous. The peaks of the distant mountains loomed ahead, shrouded in a perpetual veil of mist.

After a full day of travel, the sky was painted with the hues of sunset, casting an eerie glow on the rocky landscape. The wind had picked up, howling through the jagged rocks, carrying with it a faint, almost haunting whisper. They had encountered no other travelers, and the stillness of the land only added to the foreboding feeling that gnawed at Zephyros.

As the path began to split into two distinct directions, Zephyros pulled the reins of his horse, bringing it to a halt at the fork in the road. Elion, riding beside him, slowed as well, his sharp eyes scanning the area.

"We've come to a crossroads," Zephyros said, his voice thoughtful. "Let's see where the map leads us."

He reached into his cloak and pulled out the map Aurelius had given them, carefully unfolding it. The parchment felt oddly warm in his hands, as though imbued with magic, but Zephyros thought little of it. He studied the map closely, looking for any indication of which path to take. The markings seemed clear enough—one road led toward the distant mountains, while the other veered south toward a darker, more ominous forest.

Elion leaned closer, examining the map over Zephyros's shoulder. "The temple lies to the east beyond the mountains. We should continue along the northern route." Zephyros nodded, but something about the map caught his attention. The lines seemed to shimmer slightly, almost as if they were shifting. For a brief moment, he thought he saw the markings on the map change—faint lines bending and twisting, the paths altering. But before he could be certain, the shimmer faded, and the map appeared as it had before.

"Strange……" Zephyros muttered, frowning slightly. "This map…… Something feels off."

Elion glanced at him, sensing his unease. "What do you mean?"

"I thought I saw it shift," Zephyros replied, his brow furrowing. "As if the paths were changing."

Elion looked at the map again but saw nothing out of the ordinary. "Could be the magic Aurelius mentioned. These maps are enchanted, after all."

Zephyros hesitated for a moment but then shook his head. "Maybe. Let's take the northern path." With a final glance at the map, Zephyros folded it and tucked it back into his cloak. He nudged his horse forward, and they set off down the northern trail, the wind at their backs.

For hours, they traveled in silence, the landscape growing more rugged as they neared the foothills of the mountains. The temperature continued to drop, and the sky grew darker as clouds rolled in, casting the land in shadow. As they trekked through a narrow ravine, the hairs on the back of Zephyros's neck stood on end.

He felt it before he saw anything—the unmistakable presence of something unnatural watching them.

Elion sensed it too. His hand instinctively moved to the hilt of his sword, his gaze scanning the cliffs on either side of the ravine. "Something's not right," Elion muttered under his breath. "We're being watched."

Zephyros tightened his grip on the reins, his senses alert. He reached out with his magic, feeling the energy in the air. It was faint, but there was no mistaking it—dark magic lurking beyond sight.

Suddenly, from the shadows of the cliffs, a group of creatures emerged—twisted, unnatural beings with grotesque forms. Their bodies were covered in leathery skin, and their eyes glowed with a sickly yellow light. They moved with eerie silence, their movements swift and predatory.

The first creature lunged at Zephyros with terrifying speed, its claws extended. Zephyros reacted instinctively, raising his hand and summoning a bolt of lightning that struck the creature in midair. It screeched in agony as the electricity coursed through its body, but it wasn't enough to stop the others.

"More incoming!" Elion shouted as he drew his sword, the blade gleaming in the dim light. Two more creatures descended from the cliffs, their eyes locked on Elion. He deflected the first strike with his sword, his movements fluid and precise. With a swift counter-attack, he slashed at the creature's chest, sending it sprawling to the ground. The second creature lunged at him, but Elion sidestepped, bringing his sword down in a clean arc that severed its head from its body.

Zephyros, meanwhile, faced off against two of the creatures that had surrounded him. He called upon the power of the storm, summoning winds that whipped around him, lifting him off the ground. As the creatures lunged, Zephyros released a pulse of energy, sending them crashing into the rocks. But more were coming.

From the darkness of the ravine, more of the writhing creatures appeared, their numbers growing with each passing moment. Zephyros and Elion fought side by side, their blades and magic cutting down the creatures one by one, but the onslaught didn't relent.

"They just keep coming!" Elion shouted, slicing through another attacker.

Zephyros gritted his teeth, his magic flaring as he blasted another group with lightning. "There has to be something driving them. These creatures don't act on their own."

As the battle raged, Zephyros caught a glimpse of something in the distance—a shadowy figure, watching from the cliffs above. It was too far to make out clearly, but he could feel the malevolent presence radiating from it. Whatever it was, it was controlling the creatures, directing them toward their deaths. Zephyros's eyes narrowed.

"There's something up there," he said, pointing toward the figure. "That's our target."

Elion nodded, his eyes following Zephyros 'gaze. "Then let's finish this."

With renewed determination, the two of them fought their way through the remaining creatures, each strike bringing them closer to the figure on the cliffs. As they neared the top, the creatures began to retreat, their numbers thinning as the malevolent force withdrew.

But the battle was far from over. Zephyros and Elion climbed the last of the cliffs, reaching the top where the shadowy figure stood. Its form was humanoid but shrouded in dark robes, its face hidden beneath a hood. As they approached, the figure turned, its eyes glowing with an unnatural light. Zephyros raised his hand, ready to unleash his magic, but the figure spoke first, its voice cold and echoing.

"You are too late. The path you walk leads only to death."

Before Zephyros could respond, the figure vanished, dissolving into the shadows as if it had never been there. Elion lowered his sword, his breathing heavy. "What in the gods 'names was that?"

Zephyros frowned, his mind racing. "I don't know. But it was watching us—guiding those creatures."

Elion sheathed his sword, glancing around warily. "And the map… Something changed back there. We're being manipulated."

Zephyros nodded grimly. "The gods are playing their hand. They want us to follow this path." The air around them grew still once more, but the sense of unease lingered. Whatever force had been driving the creatures was still out there, watching, waiting.

They had no choice but to continue.

CHAPTER 25

T he sky above the Shadowed Vale was a deep indigo as Kumori and Iwa set out on their journey, the stars glittering faintly against the vast expanse of night. The wind whispered through the trees, carrying with it the scent of pine and damp earth as the two assassins moved swiftly through the dense forest, their senses attuned to the quiet sounds around them.

They had a long road ahead, and the weight of their mission—retrieving the blade of the ancient weapon hidden in the western wastelands—pressed heavily on their minds. But as capable as they were, there was one thing they didn't know. They were being followed.

Selhara, the dark elf assassin, had been trailing them since they left the Vale. Her footsteps were silent, her presence masked by the shadows themselves. A master of stealth and magic, she had been sent by

Queen Selenia to delay Kumori and Iwa, and now, as the night deepened, she was ready to strike.

The night air was still and unnervingly quiet when Kumori and Iwa finally stopped to rest. The journey had been long, and while they were both seasoned warriors, even they needed a break. Kumori crouched by the fire they had started, the flames flickering and casting long shadows around the small clearing.

"It's too quiet," he muttered, his sharp eyes scanning the surrounding trees. "I don't like it."

Iwa, sitting opposite him, grunted in agreement. "We're being watched. I've felt it for hours now." Kumori's hand drifted toward the hilt of his dagger, his senses on high alert. "Whoever it is, they're good. Too good."

He didn't have to wait long for an answer. The stillness of the night was suddenly broken by a swift, rustling sound—too fast to track. A blur of movement flashed from the shadows, and in an instant Kumori was on his feet, his daggers drawn, the firelight glinting off the polished steel.

Iwa followed suit, his feet planted firmly in the earth as he drew upon his connection to the ground beneath him, ready to unleash his power at a moment's notice.

From the shadows, Selhara emerged, her form sleek and dangerous. She moved with the grace of a predator, her twin daggers gleaming in the dim light as she approached, her silver eyes locked on the two assassins. Kumori's eyes narrowed.

"So the queen sent you, didn't she?"

Selhara smiled faintly, but her expression was cold. "Clever boy. Yes, she did. I've been watching you both for a while now."

Iwa stepped forward, his massive frame looming over her. "If you've been watching, you should know this won't end well for you."

She tilted her head slightly, her eyes glinting with amusement. "We'll see about that."

In an instant, the fight began.

Selhara moved first, her form dissolving into the shadows, disappearing from sight as if she had never been there. Kumori's eyes darted around the clearing, his ears straining to catch the faintest sound of her movements. But she was fast—faster than anyone he had ever faced. Iwa, sensing the ground beneath them shift, slammed his foot into the earth, sending a wave of force through the soil. The ground cracked and trembled, but Selhara's movements were too quick, too unpredictable.

She reappeared behind Kumori, her daggers flashing in the firelight as she struck. Kumori barely managed to block the first blow, his own daggers clashing against hers with a sharp ring of steel. The force of her attack sent him skidding back, and for the first time in a long while, Kumori felt himself on the defensive. But he wasn't one to back down easily.

With a swift movement, he retaliated, lightning crackling along the edge of his daggers as he struck back. Selhara danced around his attacks, her movements fluid and precise. She was a blur of motion, her form flickering in and out of the shadows as she closed in again.

Iwa, meanwhile, unleashed his power, the earth beneath them surging upward in jagged spikes, trying to trap Selhara in place. But she was too quick, her form dissolving into shadows once more, evading the traps with ease.

Kumori growled in frustration, his magic surging as he sent a bolt of lightning crashing toward her. The air crackled with energy as the lightning struck, but

Selhara deflected it with a flick of her wrist, her magic absorbing the blow effortlessly.

"You'll have to do better than that," she taunted, her voice carrying an edge of amusement.

The fight continued, each of them pushing the other to their limits. Selhara's skill was undeniable—she was fast, precise, and deadly. But Kumori and Iwa were nothing if not determined. Finally, after what felt like an eternity of clashing blades and surging magic, the three combatants stood at a standoff. Kumori's breath came in ragged gasps, his daggers still crackling with residual lightning. Iwa stood behind him, his fists clenched, ready for another strike. And Selhara, though equally winded, remained poised, her eyes sharp and calculating.

For a moment, none of them moved, the tension thick in the air. Selhara's smile returned, but it was less mocking this time.

"Not bad," she admitted, sheathing her daggers with a smooth motion. "You two are better than I expected."

Kumori's eyes narrowed, his grip on his weapons still tight. "What do you want?"

Selhara raised an eyebrow, her expression shifting from playful to serious. "I was sent to stop you, to delay you. But after seeing what you're capable of, I think we might have more in common than I thought."

Iwa grunted, his voice low and rumbling. "And why should we trust anything you say?"

Selhara shrugged, her eyes gleaming in the firelight. "Because I could have killed you by now if I wanted to. But I didn't. That should tell you something." Kumori and Iwa exchanged a glance, their suspicions still high, but there was truth in her words. She had held back, and now they were at an impasse. "Perhaps," Kumori said slowly, his voice cautious, "we can work together. But make no mistake—if you betray us, you won't get a second chance."

Selhara smiled, her expression unreadable. "Fair enough." The night settled around them once more, the fire crackling softly in the clearing. For now, the bloodlust has worn off, but whether Selhara would truly become an ally remained to be seen.

CHAPTER 26

The fire crackled softly in the clearing, casting flickering shadows across the forest floor as Kumori, Iwa, and Selhara settled down after their intense fight. The tension between the three had not fully dissipated, but for the moment there was a fragile truce. Iwa, ever the cautious one, sat a short distance away, his eyes never leaving Selhara. He didn't trust her—his instincts told him that she was dangerous, unpredictable. But Kumori, despite his usual wariness, was willing to listen.

Selhara leaned against a nearby tree, her form relaxed, but her sharp eyes constantly scanning the surroundings. She could feel Iwa's gaze on her, but she paid it no mind. It wasn't the first time she had been under scrutiny, and it certainly wouldn't be the last. What mattered now was the conversation at hand.

Kumori broke the silence first, his voice low and measured. "You've been following us for some time now, and you've held back. Why?"

Selhara's lips curved into a faint smile, though it didn't quite reach her eyes. "Because I wanted to see what you were capable of. I had orders to delay you, perhaps even stop you if I could. But I'm not the loyal servant the queen thinks I am."

Iwa snorted, folding his arms across his broad chest. "Then why follow her orders at all?"

Selhara's smile faded, replaced by a more serious expression. "Because I had to. The queen sent me to stop you, and the dark wizard at her side keeps a close eye on those who serve her. But I'm not loyal to her— I never was."

Kumori narrowed his eyes. "Then who are you loyal to?"

"Myself. And those I can trust." A brief silence followed as Kumori considered her words. He had seen many people claim loyalty to themselves, but there was something about the way Selhara spoke—an edge of truth that intrigued him. Still, he wasn't one to trust easily.

"What's your real agenda?" Kumori asked, his voice calm but firm.

Selhara sighed softly, her expression hardening. "Revenge." She shifted her position slightly, her eyes narrowing as memories from her past surfaced. "The queen—Selenia—she's not just a manipulative ruler. She's a murderer. She killed my family, took everything from me. And I've been waiting for the right moment to strike back. But I can't do it alone, not with that dark wizard backing her. He's powerful, more than you know."

Kumori listened in silence, his instincts telling him there was more to her story. He glanced briefly at Iwa, who remained tense but quiet, then back to Selhara. "And what do we have to do with this?"

Selhara's gaze softened slightly. "I need people I can trust. People who have the skill and the will to fight back. I've seen what you're capable of, Kumori. You're strong, resourceful. I believe you could help me—if you choose to."

Iwa finally spoke up, his voice a low growl. "You want us to help you overthrow the queen?"

Selhara shook her head. "Not yet. The queen is a powerful figure, but it's the dark wizard who makes her untouchable. If we deal with him, Selenia will fall. But I can't get close to him alone. He's too well-guarded, too paranoid. I need allies, and I need people I can trust."

Kumori raised an eyebrow. "And you think we're those people?"

Selhara's expression grew more serious. "I do. I've watched you both. I know you have your own mission, and I'm not asking you to abandon it, but once you retrieve the blade, I believe our paths will cross again. And when they do, I want us to be on the same side."

Iwa's eyes flicked to Kumori, his distrust still evident. "We don't even know if we can trust her."

Kumori was silent for a moment, weighing his options. He didn't trust easily, but he couldn't deny that Selhara's words held a certain truth. She had opportunities to kill them or hinder their progress, and yet she had chosen to engage them directly. That wasn't the mark of someone looking for a quick betrayal.

"You've told us your story, and you've asked for our help. But know this—we're not bound to you. Our mission is our priority. We'll stop in the next town, gather supplies, and continue on our journey. If we cross paths again, we'll see where things stand." Kumori said.

Selhara nodded, accepting his terms without argument. "Fair enough. I'll help you reach the blade. After that, we can discuss what comes next."

Iwa, still tense, stood and began pacing near the fire. "I don't like this," he muttered under his breath.

Kumori glanced at him, his tone softening slightly. "I know. But for now, we play along. We'll stay sharp, keep our guard up. If she tries anything, we deal with it." Iwa grunted but didn't argue. He trusted Kumori, and if Kumori thought this was the right move, he'd follow.

Selhara watched the exchange silently, her expression unreadable. She knew she had a long way to go before earning their trust, but for now this tenuous alliance was enough. The fire crackled softly between them, and for the first time in a long while, Selhara allowed herself to feel something other than bitterness.

As the night deepened, the three of them discussed their next steps. The plan was simple: head to the next town over, gather the necessary supplies, and continue their journey to retrieve the blade. The mission came first, and until it was complete, they would focus on nothing else.

But Selhara's revelation about the queen lingered in the air like a dark, oppressive force. Revenge was a powerful motivator, and while Kumori couldn't fully trust Selhara, he understood the relentless drive it brought. He had his own demons, ones that echoed in the shadows between them. Their alliance wasn't forged from trust or even shared ambition. Instead, something deeper—something unnatural—seemed to bind them. A faint, unspoken energy tethered them together, like invisible threads pulled tight by forces they didn't yet understand.

For now, they would move forward as uneasy allies, their fragile bond held together by forces lurking beyond their control, forces that neither of them dared to question—at least not yet.

As the fire burned low and the forest grew quieter, Kumori glanced up at the sky, the stars twinkling faintly overhead. The journey ahead was long, and the dangers were many. But with each step, they moved closer to their ultimate goal—the blade, the hilt, and the fate of the world. And somewhere in the darkness, the queen waited, her eyes ever-watchful. For Kumori, Iwa, and now Selhara, the real challenge was only beginning.

CHAPTER 27

The Frozen Peaks loomed ahead, their jagged summits piercing the sky like ancient spears left behind by titans. The biting wind howled through the barren landscape, whipping at Zephyros and Elion as they made their way through the harsh terrain. Snow swirled around them in thick flurries, the temperature dropping with every step they took closer to their destination.

Zephyros tightened his cloak around him, his breath visible in the frigid air as he pressed on. Elion, his sharp eyes scanning the path ahead, walked beside him in silence. They had been traveling for hours, and the weight of their mission, along with the isolation of the mountains, had left them both deep in thought.

Elion broke the silence first. "It's strange, isn't it? The further we go, the more it feels like the gods are watching us, guiding our every step."

Zephyros glanced at him, his brow furrowed. "They've been manipulating us from the start. This isn't the first time we've felt their presence, and it won't be the last."

Elion let out a low sigh, his breath clouding in the cold. "But to what end? They keep sending us in directions we don't expect, leading us to places we wouldn't go on our own. Why? What do they gain from this?"

The gods 'interference had always been a thorn in Zephyros's side—an ever-present reminder that no matter how strong he became, there were forces far beyond his control. He had spent years chasing power, seeking revenge for his family's death at the hands of those very gods, and now they seemed to be toying with him, nudging him toward their own mysterious ends.

"I don't trust them," Zephyros finally said, his voice hard. "They've always treated us like pawns in their game. They give us enough to keep us moving forward, but never the whole picture."

Elion nodded in agreement, though his gaze was distant. "I wonder what they're really after. They sent us after the hilt of this weapon, but what do they gain if we succeed? If we reach the Abyssal Depths and retrieve the weapon, we could challenge their power. Why help us?"

Zephyros's eyes darkened as he considered the question. "Maybe they think they can control us. Maybe they believe that once we have the weapon, we'll do their bidding without question."

Elion's jaw clenched. "And will we?" The question hung in the air between them, heavy and laden with uncertainty. Zephyros didn't answer right away, his mind turning over the possibilities. What would he do once they retrieved the weapon? He had always been driven by his desire for vengeance against the gods, but what would happen once he stood at the threshold of the Abyssal Depths, armed with a weapon capable of toppling them?

"I don't know," Zephyros admitted quietly, his gaze fixed on the distant peaks. "But I do know this. I won't be anyone's pawn. Not the gods', not anyone's. When the time comes, we make our own choices."

Elion's eyes narrowed slightly, though his voice remained calm. "And what if those choices lead us somewhere darker than we expect? You've felt it, haven't you? The way the gods have twisted our path—what if they're leading us straight into a trap?"

Zephyros looked at him, his expression unreadable. "We're already in a trap, Elion. The moment we agreed to seek out this weapon, we stepped into their game. But that doesn't mean we have to play it by their rules."

Elion's hand instinctively moved to the hilt of his sword, his grip tightening as old memories surfaced. "I've seen what the gods can do when they've had enough of mortals meddling in their affairs. The last time I encountered one of their kind, half a village was wiped out. And for what? A petty argument over a temple. If we challenge them, it won't be a clean fight."

Zephyros's eyes burned with quiet fury. "I'm not looking for a clean fight. I'm looking for justice—for my family, for everything they've taken from me."

Elion met his gaze, his own expression hardening. "And if it's more than justice? What if it's revenge?" The words stung, not because they were untrue, but because Zephyros had always known that revenge was the fuel that kept him moving forward. His need for vengeance against the gods had driven him for so long that it had become his purpose. But now, standing on the brink of wielding a power that could shift the balance of the world, he had to wonder if there was more to it.

"What do you want, Elion?" Zephyros asked, his voice low. "Once we reach the Abyssal Depths and retrieve this weapon, what do you plan to do with it?"

Elion's eyes softened, though the tension between them remained. "I don't know. Maybe I'll use it to protect what's left of my people, to shield them from the gods 'wrath. Or maybe I'll destroy it so no one can use it. What I do know is that we need to think beyond vengeance. The gods are dangerous, but so is unchecked power."

Zephyros held his gaze for a long moment, his own thoughts swirling with doubt. Elion wasn't wrong—unchecked power was dangerous, even in the hands of those with good intentions. But Zephyros's hatred for the gods ran deep, and he wasn't sure he could let go of the need for revenge so easily. Before either of them could speak again, a sudden gust of wind howled through the mountain pass, bringing with it a faint whisper that neither of them could quite make out.

Zephyros and Elion both stopped, their eyes scanning the area. The air had changed, carrying with it a sense of unease. "Did you hear that?" Elion asked, his voice tense.

Zephyros nodded, his hand already moving to his sword. "We're not alone."

They turned in unison, their senses heightened as the wind swirled around them. The mountains seemed to shift, the shadows deepening as an unnatural presence made itself known. Zephyros felt it first—a subtle pulse of magic, dark and malevolent, watching them from beyond the veil of reality.

"Something's coming," Zephyros murmured, his grip tightening on his blade. "And it's not friendly."

Elion drew his sword, his eyes scanning the shadows. "The gods?"

"Perhaps," Zephyros replied, his voice low. "Or something worse."

As the wind howled and the air grew colder, the gods 'influence over their journey became painfully clear. They were being led, manipulated, every step of the way. And now, whatever awaited them in the Frozen Peaks was no coincidence.

And as the shadows closed in, Zephyros and Elion knew they had no choice but to face it head-on.

CHAPTER 28

The journey from the Shadowed Vale to the Radiant Plains had been long and arduous, but Varun had never been one to shy away from such trials. The stark contrast between the two realms was not lost on him. Where the Vale was cloaked in shadows, secrets, and the ever-present hum of ancient magic, the Radiant Plains gleamed with an overwhelming brightness that felt almost oppressive.

As Varun crested the final hill, the first city of the Radiant Plains came into view. Auradale, a place known for its beauty and its connection to the gods of light, stretched out before him like a vast tapestry of gold and white. The sun hung high in the sky, its light reflecting off the alabaster buildings, casting the streets in a perpetual glow that seemed almost otherworldly.

But as Varun entered the city, it was clear that he was out of place. The streets were bustling with people, their clothes bright and colorful, their faces open and unguarded. Children ran through the squares, laughing, while merchants called out to passersby, their stalls overflowing with vibrant fabrics, polished jewels, and fragrant spices. There was an energy here, one of joy and peace, that Varun found almost unsettling.

His dark cloak, tattered and stained with the dust of travel, marked him as different. His skin, weathered and shadowed, stood in stark contrast to the bright, radiant faces of the locals. As he passed through the streets, the people parted, their eyes following him with a mixture of curiosity, disdain, and fear.

Whispers followed him like a shadow.

"Who is he?"

"Does he come from the Shadowed Vale?"

"A dark one, here? He'll bring nothing but trouble."

Varun kept his gaze forward, his expression unreadable as he strode through the streets. He was used to such reactions. The people of the Radiant Plains had always viewed the Vale with suspicion, seeing it as a place of darkness and mystery. And while they revered Clerus as one of their greatest protectors, they rarely extended that reverence to his old friends.

As Varun continued through the city, the grand silhouette of Clerus's temple began to rise before him. It was impossible to miss—an awe-inspiring structure that dominated the skyline, its towering spires reaching toward the heavens. The temple, known as the Sanctum of Light, was unlike anything Varun had ever seen, even in his travels through the realms.

The temple stood on a raised platform, its white marble steps gleaming under the sunlight. At the base, the foundation was carved with intricate designs, depicting the history of the gods and their champions. Figures of light were locked in battle with dark forces, their forms captured in a way that made them seem almost alive, frozen in eternal conflict.

The walls of the temple were made of pristine white stone, polished to a reflective sheen that caught the sunlight, making the entire structure appear as if it were glowing from within. But it was the stained glass windows that drew Varun's gaze.

Each window, reaching nearly from the ground to the towering archways above, was a masterpiece in its own right. The glass was a kaleidoscope of colors—deep blues, radiant golds, fiery reds, and emerald greens—depicting scenes from the ancient texts.

Angels with wings of light, champions of the gods wielding weapons of power, and the gods themselves, standing in judgment over the world. The artistry was immaculate, each detail painstakingly crafted to reflect the glory of the divine.

And as the sun hit the glass, light poured through the windows, casting brilliant, multicolored beams across the courtyard. The light seemed to dance on the ground, illuminating the faces of the people who approached the temple, casting them in a divine glow. To those who lived in Auradale, this was a place of salvation, a beacon of hope in a world that sometimes seemed too dark to bear. But for Varun, the light felt almost suffocating.

The great doors of the temple were made of solid gold, etched with the sigils of the gods, and flanked by two towering statues of winged figures—guardians of the temple, forever watching. As Varun approached, the doors opened with a low, resonant sound, revealing the interior of the sanctum.

Inside, the grandeur continued. The walls were lined with more stained glass, and the ceiling stretched high above, painted with images of celestial beings and stars. The air was warm, filled with the faint scent of incense and the soft murmur of prayer. And at the far end of the temple, seated on a raised dais, was Clerus.

Clerus, High Cleric of Radiant Plains, was a man of immense power and presence. His robes were pure white, lined with threads of gold that shimmered in the light. His skin was fair, almost glowing, and his hair, once dark, had turned silver with age, though his eyes were as sharp as ever. He held a staff, its top adorned with a glimmering crystal that pulsed with divine energy, and as Varun approached, those sharp eyes met his.

For a long moment, neither spoke. Varun finally broke the silence, his voice low and steady. "It's been a long time, old friend."

Clerus stood, his presence commanding, but there was warmth in his expression. "Too long, Varun. Much has changed since you last walked these halls."

Varun nodded, his gaze briefly drifting to the stained glass once more. "And yet some things remain the same."

Clerus stepped down from the dais, approaching Varun with measured steps. "You didn't come all this way to admire the architecture. What brings you here?"

Varun's eyes darkened, his thoughts heavy with the knowledge he had uncovered. "I've uncovered something, Clerus. Something that could change everything. And I need your help."

Clerus raised an eyebrow, his expression becoming more serious. "Tell me."

As the two old friends stood in the center of the temple, the light from the stained glass casting vibrant colors across their faces, Varun knew that the conversation they were about to have would shape the course of the future—for both the Radiant Plains and the Shadowed Vale. And perhaps for the gods themselves.

CHAPTER 29

The soft light from the stained glass windows bathed the grand hall in a kaleidoscope of colors, but the weight of the conversation between Varun and Clerus cast a shadow that no amount of light could dispel. Varun stood across from his old friend, the warmth of their reunion giving way to the gravity of the situation.

Clerus, ever composed, listened as Varun explained everything—his voice measured but urgent. "Kumori and Zephyros are heading toward their respective goals. The pieces of the weapon are scattered, but that's not the only concern."

Varun's eyes darkened as he spoke of the revelations he uncovered in the Dark Library. "I found something about Aethas in the archives. He's not just any chosen one. The weapon isn't a sword. It's a spear, and the wielder of that spear is destined to take control of the Abyssal Depths. The gods know. They must know by now. They've been manipulating events for their own ends, but this goes deeper than we thought."

Clerus's face remained impassive as Varun continued, though his sharp eyes revealed that he understood the gravity of the situation. "The shaft of the spear," Varun said, pacing slightly as he spoke, "it's missing. I need to either find it or create it, but I don't know where to start."

At this, Clerus tilted his head slightly, his fingers gently tapping the staff he held.

"You're right, Varun. This is no simple weapon. The spear of the Abyss is a conduit, a tool of immense power. And like all great weapons, it must be forged with purpose."

Varun stopped pacing, focusing on Clerus.

"The shaft," Clerus said "must be made from a rare material, one that's almost impossible to acquire. It's known as orikal—a metal found only in the deepest reaches of the planet, where the pressure is immense and the heat unbearable. Only a few fragments of it remain in the world. Even if you find it, the process of forging it into the shaft won't be easy."

Varun's brow furrowed. He had heard of orikal before, whispered in the darkest of circles. "Where do I begin?"

Clerus took a deep breath, his gaze piercing. "You don't only need orikal. The shaft itself must be infused with the power of the wielder—Aethas. The spear will only respond to him, for he is its true master. His essence, his magic, must be intertwined with the material as it's forged."

Varun's eyes narrowed in thought. "Infusing it with Aethas 'power? That means…he'll need to be there when it's made."

Clerus nodded. "Yes. It won't be an easy task, and it will require great precision. Aethas is young and still discovering his potential, but the Abyss chose him for a reason. His power, whether he understands it or not, is connected to the spear. Only he can wield it, and only his magic can awaken the full potential of the weapon."

Varun's mind raced. Finding orikal was one challenge, but infusing it with Aethas's power would be another. The boy was still training, still learning. Time was running short.

Clerus took a step forward, his voice softening slightly. "There's more." Varun looked up, sensing the shift in Clerus 'tone.

"I've heard whispers," Clerus continued, "whispers of the gods 'true intentions. They know what's happening, Varun, and they're not sitting idly by. They've been moving pieces on the board long before you and I even realized it. And while the spear is powerful, it's not the only weapon they've placed in this game."

Varun's expression darkened. "What do you mean?"

"There's another weapon, a set of daggers. They're made from the same material as the spear shaft, but their edges are infused with pure lightning, capable of cutting through even the most powerful magic. The gods placed these daggers in the world long ago, but their purpose remains unclear. Whoever wields them…"

Varun's heart skipped a beat as his thoughts immediately turned to Kumori. He had seen the way Kumori wielded lightning with terrifying precision, how the clouds themselves seemed to respond to his will.

"Those daggers," Varun said, his voice low, "they belong to Kumori."

Clerus nodded slightly. "It's possible. He's the one with the connection to the storm, to lightning. The gods may have destined him to find them, as Aethas is destined to wield the spear. But why would the gods place such powerful weapons in the hands of mortals? That's the question we must answer."

Varun's fists clenched at his sides. The gods were playing a dangerous game, manipulating events to their advantage. The pieces were falling into place, but the purpose behind it all was still shrouded in mystery.

"They're setting us all up for something," Varun muttered, frustrated, "but I won't let them control us."

Clerus watched Varun for a moment, his eyes filled with understanding. "That's why you must be prepared. The gods won't stop. They'll continue to manipulate, to guide, to control, until they get what they want. But you, Varun, you're not bound to their will. You still have the power to shape your own path."

Varun took a deep breath, his mind racing with everything he had learned. The spear, the daggers, Aethas, Kumori—their fates were all intertwined. The gods were positioning them for something greater, something that could reshape the very fabric of the world.

"Thank you, Clerus," Varun said quietly, his voice steady once more. "I'll find the orikal, and I'll bring Aethas to you when the time is right. But first I need to ensure that Kumori understands what he's up against."

Clerus placed a hand on Varun's shoulder, his expression somber. "Be careful, old friend. The gods are watching, and their reach extends further than we know." Varun nodded, a sense of resolve filling him.

The path ahead was perilous, but he would not be swayed. He had his mission, and he would see it through—no matter the cost.

As he turned to leave the temple, the stained glass cast long shadows across the floor, the light shifting as if in response to the decisions being made. Varun didn't look back, his mind focused on the task ahead. The game was in motion, and the stakes had never been higher.

CHAPTER 30

The Shadowed Vale welcomed Varun back with its familiar silence, the shadows clinging to him like old companions. The journey from the Radiant Plains had been swift, but his mind was weighed down by the gravity of what he had learned from Clerus. As he walked through the ancient stone corridors, his thoughts were consumed with the task ahead—finding the orikal, forging the spear, and preparing Aethas for his destiny.

Upon entering the heart of the Vale, Varun was greeted by Velkar, his second-in-command, and Enilcmai. Both men inclined their heads in acknowledgment of his return, though their expressions carried a certain weight that immediately caught Varun's attention.

"Varun," Velkar said, his voice measured but laced with curiosity, "you'll want to hear what's happened since you left."

Without missing a beat, Enilcmai added, "Aethas has progressed faster than we expected."

Varun's eyes narrowed slightly, a mixture of surprise and concern washing over him. "Faster? How so?"

Enilcmai exchanged a brief glance with Velkar before continuing. "He's been training nonstop, mastering control over the wind like nothing I've ever seen. He can conjure blasts of air powerful enough to knock down stone, and he's learned to ride the wind itself. His speed… I've barely been able to keep up with him during our sparring sessions."

Varun's brow furrowed. He had known that Aethas held great potential, but this level of progress was astonishing. The boy was tapping into the power of the Abyss far sooner than Varun had anticipated.

"He's become formidable, but…" Enilcmai hesitated for a moment. "I sense a growing hunger in him. The power excites him, and he's pushing himself harder than he should."

Varun nodded thoughtfully, understanding the concern. Power, especially of this magnitude, could be intoxicating, and Aethas was still young. It would be easy for him to lose himself in the thrill of it, especially with his destiny looming over him.

"I'll speak with him," Varun said. "First, I need to tell you both what I've learned."

As Varun approached the training grounds, he found Aethas sitting near the edge of the field, breathing heavily after another round of intense training. His eyes glowed faintly with that familiar emerald light, and a light breeze seemed to swirl around him even in his moments of rest.

"Aethas," Varun called, his voice steady but carrying an undercurrent of authority, "you've done well today. Clean up and rest for now. We'll talk later."

Aethas looked up, his expression filled with both pride and exhaustion. "But I can still keep going—"

"Rest," Varun said firmly, cutting him off. "You'll need your strength for what's coming." The young man reluctantly nodded, standing and heading toward the nearby quarters. But as he walked away, his curiosity got the better of him. Using the wind, Aethas allowed the voices of Varun, Enilcmai, and Velkar to drift toward him, carried on the gentle breeze that followed him everywhere. In the meeting chamber, Varun stood before Enilcmai and Velkar, his expression grim as he began to recount his journey to the Radiant Plains.

"I spoke with Clerus," Varun began, his voice low but filled with purpose. "What I found in the Dark Library was only part of the truth. The weapon Aethas is meant to wield isn't a sword—it's a spear. The spear of the Abyss, and its wielder will not only open the Abyssal Depths but take control of it." He paused, letting the weight of his words sink in.

"Aethas is that wielder," Varun continued. "He is the one destined to rule the Abyss and lead its disciples. The gods know this, and they're moving against us. We must be prepared."

Enilcmai's expression remained stoic, though there was a flicker of concern in his eyes. "And the spear?"

Varun nodded. "The shaft is missing. It must be forged from orikal—a rare material found deep within the Earth. Clerus told me where we might find it, but it won't be easy to retrieve."

"The next part," Varun said, his tone growing more intense. "The shaft must be infused with Aethas's essence, his magic. Only then will the spear be whole, and only then will he be able to unlock its full potential." There was a heavy silence in the room, broken only by the faint sound of the wind rustling through the nearby trees.

"And there's something else," Varun added, his voice dropping to a whisper. "Clerus spoke of another weapon, a set of daggers. They're made from the same material as the spear, but their edges are pure lightning, capable of cutting through even the strongest magic. Kumori must be the one destined to wield them."

Enilcmai raised an eyebrow. "Kumori, the one with lightning in his veins."

Varun nodded. "The gods are playing a dangerous game, and they've placed these weapons in the world for a reason. We need to find the orikal and complete the spear before it's too late."

Enilcmai stood, his powerful form casting a shadow across the chamber. "I'll take someone and retrieve the orikal. If we delay any longer, the gods may act before we're ready."

But before Varun could respond, a voice rang out from the doorway, carried on the wind. "I'm coming with you."

All three men turned to see Aethas standing in the entrance, his eyes blazing. The wind seemed to swirl around him as if responding to his emotions, his aura brimming with power.

"You heard us," Varun said quietly, though it was more a statement than a question.

Aethas stepped forward, his expression unwavering. "I'm ready. If I'm supposed to be the one to wield this spear, then I need to be strong enough to defend myself, to lead. I won't sit here and wait while you go off to get what I need. I'm coming with you." Varun's gaze hardened, a flicker of both pride and apprehension passing through him. He had expected this, feared this, and now it had come to pass. Aethas was eager, driven, but he was also still learning the true depths of his power. Sending him into danger could either temper him or break him.

"You don't know what you're asking for," Varun said. "The orikal is hidden in dangerous places. You may not be ready."

Aethas clenched his fists. "Then let me prove that I am. I need to do this."

Varun studied him for a long moment, seeing the fire in the young man's eyes. The Abyss had chosen him for a reason. And if Aethas truly was destined to rule it, then he would need to face danger. Perhaps this was the only way to truly test his mettle.

Finally, Varun nodded. "Very well. If you are truly the ruler of the Abyss, then you should be able to defend yourself. But once you step onto this path, there is no turning back. You will face trials that will test your strength, your will, and your very soul."

Aethas's gaze never wavered. "I understand. And I'm ready."

Varun exchanged a look with Enilcmai, who gave a curt nod. The decision had been made. "The journey begins now," Varun said, his voice low but filled with resolve. "Gather your strength, for what lies ahead will define us all."

As Aethas turned to leave, the wind at his back, he couldn't help but feel the weight of the future pressing down on him. But there was excitement too, and with it the promise of a chance to prove himself.

He imagined the spear made of this mythical metal, tried to envision holding it in his hands. "Could I really wield such a weapon? Could I rule the Abyss?"